Hamstermagic

H o LLY WEBB

SCHOLASTIC INC.

New York   Toronto   London   Auckland
Sydney   Mexico City   New Delhi   Hong Kong

For Jon, Tom, Robin, and William

ISBN: 978-0-545-16053-7

Text copyright © 2009 by Holly Webb

All rights reserved. Published by Scholastic Inc., 557 Broadway, New York, NY 10012, by arrangement with Scholastic Ltd. SCHOLASTIC, APPLE PAPERBACKS, and associated logos are trademarks and/or registered trademarks of Scholastic Inc.

12 11 10 9 8 7 6 5 4 3 2   10 11 12 13 14 15/0

Printed in the U.S.A.
First U.S. edition, February 2010

1

"I am glad I do not have to go out," Sofie said smugly, peering out at the dark street. She gave a luxurious little shiver, setting her big dachshund ears quivering, and yawned. "Put on your scarf, Lottie. Fog is very bad for the chest." She settled herself more comfortably on her purple velvet cushion, wrapping her smooth black tail tightly around her bottom as though she was afraid of drafts. She looked very much like an indoor dog, Lottie thought enviously, with her polished black coat and delicate ginger eyebrows.

Lottie looked out the window at the misty swirls wreathing the lamppost and shivered. It was only the third week of October, but autumn had come in with a vengeance. She picked up her backpack and winced — she was sure it felt lighter when the weather was sunny. "Bye, Uncle Jack!" she called through to the kitchen at the back of the shop.

Her uncle wandered out to wave good-bye, crunching a piece of toast, and Lottie gave him a rather resentful look. He still had his slippers on. It just wasn't fair. Still, she had to go. She was supposed to be meeting Ruby halfway to school.

"Come home quickly after school, Lottie," Uncle Jack reminded her thickly through a mouthful of peanut butter. "Interesting new delivery coming today, from that supplier down on the coast. New mice, I think!"

Lottie nodded, feeling a little more cheerful. She had been living at her uncle's pet shop for nearly four months, while her mother was abroad. Lottie's mum worked in Paris now, since her company had transferred her to their French office. It had been a huge upheaval for Lottie to leave all her friends and stay with Uncle Jack and Danny for summer vacation, and she'd been furious about it.

She'd been even more upset when her mum had told her that it wouldn't be just a few weeks in Netherbridge as she'd expected. The French job had been extended, and Lottie would have to start the new school year in Netherbridge. But she loved the shop now — so much so that she couldn't imagine going home again. The shop was full of the most amazing magical creatures, most of whom talked, and Uncle Jack kept finding new ones. New animals were always exciting, and the mice were some of the funniest creatures they had.

As she opened the shop door, she heard her favorite pink mice starting to argue about where the new mice's cage would go. "Next to us!" they were pleading with Uncle Jack. "Can't you move Septimus's cage? He's always at school with Danny, anyway — we hardly ever see him."

Septimus was a black rat who'd overcome his habitual laziness to accompany Lottie's cousin to school. Danny was in his first year at the junior high school, and hated it. He'd been very lonely at first, but he was far too proud to admit it. Septimus, who adored him, had volunteered to keep him company if sufficiently bribed with peanut brittle. Together they seemed to be plotting a takeover of the teachers' lounge, but at least Danny seemed a bit happier at school.

Grace's Pet Shop was in the middle of one of the main shopping streets in Netherbridge, but the whole town was old-fashioned, with narrow roads, lots of cobblestones, and pretty bridges over the river. At this end of the street, the black-and-white timbered houses leaned closer together over the road, the walls bulging, as though the houses were half alive. Lottie sniffed the air as she set off down the street. It was slightly sour, and smoky.

Netherbridge looked like something out of a television show, the kind where everyone wore big frilly petticoats. She expected a carriage and horses to gallop down the street beside her, the coachman yelling at his team of horses, hurrying them along to escape the highwaymen. The coiling mist thickened, just like a special effect, and Lottie listened for the thunder of hooves. Or maybe a vampire ought to glide out from one of those dark alleyways. She moved slightly farther into the middle of the street.

Lottie shivered, and shook herself. Why was she letting the mist get to her like this? It was just weather, nothing spooky about it. Still, she caught her breath when figures started to approach her out of the grayish fog, especially as one did seem to be wrapped in a long black cloak, just like bat wings. . . .

"Nonsense! Absolute nonsense! A myth!" one of them said.

Lottie sighed out a shaky breath of relief. Vampires didn't talk like that. Probably, anyway. Lottie added vampires to her mental list of things to ask Uncle Jack about. Dragons had turned out to be real, after all, even though the pair she knew were only cat-sized.

The misty figures turned into two solid men, one tall, one extremely short, and both arguing.

"I tell you, I saw it! Running around on Netherbridge Hill! Horn a foot long!" The little man was getting so mad that his face had turned scarlet, and the mist looked like steam billowing from his ears.

"Sssshhh!" His companion had noticed Lottie approaching and obviously didn't want to be overheard.

"Stop fussing, you overgrown beanpole, it's only Jack Grace's girl. Whatsername. Lily." The short one peered through the fog at Lottie. "Lara? Lucy?"

"Lottie," said Lottie, giggling.

"Lottie. Exactly. Like I said. Did you know there was a unicorn up on Netherbridge Hill, Louisa?"

Lottie shook her head, not sure whether to believe him or not. She recognized him now — Mr. Fieldfare, who came to the shop sometimes to buy birdseed. He lived up north somewhere, but Grace's was one of the few magic pet shops in the country, so many of the customers traveled a long way for their supplies. Mr. Fieldfare had a flock of brilliantly colored finches flying free in his house, Uncle Jack said. Mr. Fieldfare didn't call them finches, though — he always spoke of them as his feathered jewels.

"This is Jacob, Laura, my old friend Jacob Bucklebank. Staying with me for Halloween, you see. Had to come down here to the shop to get some special treats for my darlings, for the celebration."

Mr. Bucklebank bowed very low, sweeping off his big black hat. He had flowing dark hair and a dark, silky beard. Mr. Fieldfare was what Uncle Jack called a financial wizard, which — as far as Lottie understood it — was a mixture of being good with money and a little extra magical something. But he didn't *look* very magical. Lottie found it hard to imagine magicians being short and fat. By contrast, his friend gave off an air of spells bubbling at his fingertips.

They waved to her, continuing their friendly squabble as they strolled on through the fog, and left Lottie wondering.

She'd only been living at the shop since July, the beginning of the summer vacation, but it hadn't taken her more than a couple of weeks to realize that it wasn't an ordinary shop. People came to it from all over the country. They came to buy Uncle Jack's amazing homemade remedies and to ask him about their problems with bad-tempered tortoises and cats who couldn't spell. There were a lot of local customers too. But most of them had no idea what was really in the cages that looked empty. They never saw the pink mice or Horace the parrot doing the crossword. They didn't know about the magic.

"Lottie!" Ruby was waving to her from the bridge. "Come on, we're going to be late!"

Lottie checked her watch — Ruby was right, she must have slowed down in the mist more than she'd realized. "Sorry!" she called, running over. The fog was thinner on the bridge. Ruby's red hair gleamed through it, and she looked reassuringly normal and not at all spooky.

"Horrible weather, isn't it?" she said cheerfully as they set off along River Street. "Just right for school. I really can't stand Mondays. Having PE on Monday morning is just cruel."

They joined the stream of children heading for the school gates, and Lottie couldn't talk to Ruby about what she'd been thinking, for fear of being overheard. Ruby had no magical powers herself, but she was a good friend and Lottie had told her the truth about what the pet shop really was. Ruby had also seen her and Sofie working magic — as Lottie's familiar, Sofie strengthened her powers and their minds were linked too. Although Ruby couldn't do that sort of thing, she'd helped Lottie with a spell here at school only a couple of weeks ago, and Lottie liked that there was at least one "normal" person in her life whom she could talk to about homework and TV instead of herbs and how to stop mice from misbehaving.

Lottie and Ruby headed for one of the benches up against the wall of the school, hoping for some shelter.

"I need to find some gloves," Lottie muttered. "Mum sent a package of clothes for me from France, and they're gorgeous, but I wish I had all my old things too. Lots of my winter stuff is packed away in storage, now that she's rented out our old apartment." She sighed, thinking of her favorite pink fluffy gloves lying at the bottom of a box somewhere.

"Is she coming back anytime soon?" Ruby asked.

Lottie shook her head. "Her bosses keep her really busy. She even has to work on weekends a lot of the time. But she thinks she might be able to come over on the train for a weekend, in a few weeks' time."

Ruby nodded sympathetically. Her mother was an artist, and even though she worked in her studio out in the backyard, sometimes she might as well be on the other side of the world. Ruby was used to getting her own dinner. But at least she could see her mum whenever she wanted.

"Ah well," Ruby said, fluttering her eyelashes. "If your mum hadn't had to go to Paris, you'd never have met *me*."

Lottie rolled her eyes and swatted Ruby with her English homework. She'd been too busy helping Uncle Jack make a batch of his special sugar mice to do it last night. Actually, she just hated writing poems, because

hers always sounded stupid. It didn't make any difference how long she spent doing it.

"Oh my word," Ruby muttered, staring across the
playground. "What is Zara Martin wearing?"

Zara and her little clique had just strolled into the
playground, ignoring everyone else.

"She looks like she has a stuffed cat on her head,"
Lottie giggled. Then she gave Ruby a horrified look.
"You don't think that's real fur, do you?"

Ruby looked thoughtfully at Zara, now modeling her
new fur hat for the rest of the girls in their class. "No,"
she said at last. "Zara wouldn't put a dead animal on
her head. Last year she wouldn't even touch our class
hamster. She hates animals."

Lottie nodded disgustedly. She'd met Zara a couple
of times during summer vacation and disliked her
before she'd even found out they were in the same
class. She and Sofie had rescued a skinny little stray
cat from Zara and her gang (though Sofie now refused
to admit that she had any part in this — she was not a
cat fan), which just made Zara more of an enemy.
Lottie had taken the cat back to the shop, half reluctantly. She hadn't been sure what Uncle Jack would say
about letting a starved little stray who couldn't talk
live with his magical animals. But Tabitha had turned

out to have magical powers of her own, and Lottie found her a wonderful home with Ariadne, as her new familiar.

"Are you doing anything for Halloween?" Lottie asked Ruby.

"No. My mum can't be bothered with all that Halloween stuff. She makes us all sit in the living room with the curtains drawn and pretend we're out. I mean, she'd probably let me go to a Halloween party, but she doesn't like trick-or-treating. She says it's all just made up to sell things. Why, anyway? Do you want to go?"

"No." Lottie wasn't sure what to say. She didn't want to sound stupid. "I went trick-or-treating last year with friends from my old school. I don't mind not doing it this year. It's just that I couldn't help feeling, this morning, that Halloween might be a bit, well, *spooky*."

Ruby looked at her as if she was silly. "What — are you worried someone might give you a nasty bite with their plastic vampire teeth?" she asked, grinning.

Lottie stared at her fingers and muttered quietly, "But what if it's not all plastic?"

"Oh!" Ruby's smile faded. "Oh, I see what you mean."

"Everyone dresses up, and it's fun and silly and not

really scary. But what if the things they're dressing up as are real?" Lottie asked.

"I hadn't thought of it like that," Ruby admitted.

"Halloween's more than just candy and pumpkins. And we know witches really exist."

"Well, of course we do, you *are* one," Ruby pointed out.

Lottie shook her head firmly. "I'm only Ariadne's apprentice. I don't know what I'm doing with most magic yet. That settles it. I'm staying indoors and watching TV this Saturday. Even if I get invited to the best Halloween party ever!"

The mist had cleared by the time they walked home from school, leaving a beautiful, crisp October day, but Lottie's unease still lingered. She *was* a witch. Ariadne had said so, after the spell Lottie had cast on Zara a couple of weeks ago. Zara had tried to set Lottie up and make it look as though she'd cheated on a test, and Lottie had protected herself with a spell. Until then, she'd been too nervous to do a spell on her own. She was actually grateful to Zara, in a weird sort of way. And she wasn't scared of her anymore. Lottie still didn't like her, but the spell had broken the hold Zara had over Lottie.

Ruby said that it was a big waste now that everyone else in the class had forgotten it had happened, but Lottie wasn't so sure. Zara didn't have the same power over the class as she'd had before. Her own little gang still followed her around like puppies, but some of the other girls had dared to stand up to her recently. It was as though Lottie's spell had broken the one that Zara had over them too.

Lottie blinked and stopped still in the middle of the sidewalk. Ruby had gone home, so luckily she was alone to think this out. *Zara's* spell? Lottie hadn't really meant that Zara was a witch, too — but was there any reason why she shouldn't be? She'd certainly had some strange, almost unnatural hold over everyone else in Lottie's class.

Lottie walked on slowly. No. Zara couldn't be. Lottie would have felt it when she used the spell. And Zara wouldn't have been so scared, because she'd have known what Lottie was doing. Possibly Zara had some power, deep down, that she used for bullying and manipulating other people, without realizing what it was. But she wasn't really magical. Lottie breathed a shaky sigh of relief. The idea of Zara as a witch was just too much. She was bad enough as she was. Magic had been fun for Lottie so far, most of the time. Zara would ruin it.

Lottie scowled as she pushed open the shop door. She didn't want to think about that kind of thing.

Sofie ran across the shop to meet her, weaving in and out of her legs with pleasure. Usually she was a very dignified little dog, but she did occasionally let her good manners lapse. Even though Sofie said she hated the idea of school, Lottie knew that what she really hated was that they had to be apart for most of the day. She and Lottie could read each other's minds, but it wasn't the same as being together.

Lottie picked Sofie up, and Sofie gave a huge yawn, suddenly remembering to be sophisticated. "School — nothing happened, as usual?" she asked, flapping a paw vaguely.

"Lottie! Perfect timing!" Uncle Jack sounded excited. He was standing by the counter, just starting to open a big cardboard pet carrier box. "The new mouse shipment has just been delivered. Very rare and interesting apparently."

"Not as rare as us?" one of the pink mice asked anxiously, climbing through his cage door and peering over from the edge of the shelf. "I'm ever so interesting," he added importantly, starting to scurry down the shelf toward the counter. "Even more than the others — they're asleep, which is really just boring, isn't it?"

"You're the most interesting mouse I know, Fred," Lottie told him reassuringly, stroking his soft rose-petal fur with one finger.

"Really?" he asked delightedly. "Even more than Henrietta?"

This was a tricky one, as Henrietta the homing mouse was quite remarkable. She didn't live in a group, like the pink mice or the shy, pink-eyed white ones. She was a lone operator. Uncle Jack sold her to people he thought didn't deserve pets, and then a few days later she would come back, having thoroughly turned her new owners off pet ownership. Whenever Lottie had seen her, she'd been a very pretty cocoa-powder brown, like a little furry truffle, but she had a variety of disguises. "Henrietta is clever, but you have character," Lottie said solemnly.

"Oh!" Fred the mouse twirled his whiskers shyly, rather overcome. He skittered up Lottie's arm to perch on her shoulder, watching Uncle Jack unfasten the box.

Sofie jumped down, yawning again. "Mice, huh! Why such a fuss? Wake me if they really are interesting," she muttered from her cushion, turning around and tucking her nose more comfortably between her paws. Lottie could feel her in the back of her mind, already deep in a warm, soft, velvety doze.

Lottie stood on tiptoe to peer into the box as Uncle Jack lifted up the flaps, and Fred teetered on Lottie's shoulder as he leaned over to look too.

"Oh!" Uncle Jack frowned.

"That's not a mouse," Fred said, sounding rather disgusted. "I don't know *what* it is."

In a ball of crumpled paper bedding, a fat orange-and-white creature was curled up, fast asleep and snoring.

"There must have been a mix-up," Uncle Jack said. "I definitely didn't order a hamster. I'll have to send it back."

"Can *we* see?" a silky voice purred from the edge of the counter, and Lottie jumped as Selina and Sarafan, the black cats, suddenly appeared on either side of the box, their whiskers twitching with excitement. Lottie was sure that Selina was drooling.

"How did you two get out?" Uncle Jack demanded, patting his pockets. "Sarafan, did you steal my keys again?" Uncle Jack didn't like shutting any of the animals up, but Selina and Sarafan couldn't be trusted around the mice. Now that they'd learned how to open latches, he was forced to padlock their enormous pen.

"If you don't want this furry thing . . ." Sarafan suggested meaningfully.

"We haven't had any exercise," Selina agreed, poking her nose into the box, her whiskers brushing the orange fur. Lottie could see all of her teeth.

"Selina, no!" Uncle Jack snapped. "This isn't a cat toy." He tried to hold Selina and Sarafan away, but they were even harder to keep hold of than ordinary cats and seemed to flow around his fingers, ending up with their front paws on the edge of the box.

"It *looks* like one," Selina purred.

At this point, the gently snoring orange ball woke up.

Lottie had been expecting that a hamster's reaction to a cat only a nose length away would be similar to a mouse's. Fred was currently cowering inside her cardigan. But the hamster opened his beady black eyes and blinked sleepily. Then the eyes sparkled, like little black diamonds, and he sat up. "Harrumph! Haven't been introduced. Most irregular. Very rude to invade a gentleman's privacy, particularly when asleep. An English hamster's bedding is his castle, and all that!"

Then he bit Selina on the nose.

Lottie couldn't help laughing. She'd never seen Selina move so fast. The two black cats were back in their pen in the far room in seconds, sulking in private.

The hamster looked up hopefully. "I don't suppose you would have any sunflower seeds to take the taste away, would you? Cat is so rancid, particularly that sort of underbred feline."

There was a hissing gasp from the cats' pen and the hamster winked at Lottie.

Uncle Jack filled a small china bowl with sunflower seeds and put it on the counter. "Would you prefer to stay in the box, or may I lift you out?" he asked politely.

"Oh, out, please," the hamster replied. "Must inspect the new quarters, what?"

Uncle Jack put a hand into the box and the hamster waddled onto it. He was rather portly but it suited him, Lottie thought. He was a very dignified little creature. He stepped onto the counter and looked approvingly at the bowl. "Very nice. Wedgewood?" he asked, running a paw over the pattern.

"Er, yes, I think so." Uncle Jack blinked. He didn't like boring brown food bowls and tended to buy little china bowls for the animals' seed mixes whenever he saw them in junk shops. But he'd never had an animal in the shop who could discuss china patterns. Lottie noticed that Uncle Jack seemed to have forgotten about sending the hamster back.

"Do excuse me," the hamster said, and bowed apologetically. "Those little scalawags have made me forget my manners. My name is Giles."

Lottie half curtsyed and Uncle Jack bowed his head politely. Giles had that effect. "I'm Jack Grace, owner of the shop, and this is my niece, Lottie. Er . . . how do you do? Was it a tiring journey?"

"Not at all, not at all," Giles replied through several sunflower seeds. He eyed Lottie interestedly, with his head on one side. "Lottie? So you'd be Lottie Grace then, would you? Mmm. I've heard of you."

2

"Heard of me?" Lottie repeated, staring at Giles in confusion.

"Yes, and not in the most flattering way, I'm afraid." Giles munched a sunflower seed, staring thoughtfully at her.

"But . . . I don't understand," Lottie faltered.

"Well, your uncle bought me from an animal importer, you see. Horrible place, not at all the sort of animals I like to associate with. Low morals. A lot of cats."

Uncle Jack looked apologetic. "I hadn't used them before. I had heard they were rather good, but perhaps I won't order from them again."

"I wouldn't." Giles nodded approvingly. "The owner was a most unpleasant man and I did not like the clientele. I have to admit, I was somewhat worried about this shop. But you seem quite respectable after all."

Lottie and Uncle Jack exchanged a glance, half

relieved, half amused. Neither of them wanted to be disapproved of by a hamster.

"So was it one of the customers who was talking about me?" Lottie asked curiously.

"Mmm. She bought two salukis. I think she'd had them specially brought from Egypt. Very valuable dogs — it was an important order." Giles shuddered. "Horrible things. So skinny, it was unnatural. And they had hungry eyes," he added darkly. "The woman who bought them must have been a friend of the owner's. They talked for a long time. They didn't seem to care that I could hear them, but the sort of things they were saying — *ugh*." He looked up at Lottie. "She didn't like you at all, Lottie. I would do my best to avoid that one if I were you." He ate another sunflower seed for comfort. "Particularly if those dogs are with her."

Lottie nodded and looked at Uncle Jack. His face was oddly blank, as though he knew something she didn't and had no intention of telling her what. "You know who it is, don't you?" she asked him.

Uncle Jack shrugged. "I think so. I imagine it's the enchantress who came into the shop a few weeks ago." He sniffed disgustedly.

"Did you *know* her?" Lottie stared at him. "You didn't say!"

"I'm not saying now." Uncle Jack folded his lips tightly and stared out the window.

"Which means you do," Lottie observed, and watched his eyebrows twitch with irritation. "Was she wearing a red dress, this woman who bought the salukis?" she asked Giles. "Long blond hair, almost white?"

"That's the one," Giles mumbled with his mouth full. "Nasty piece of work. You stay out of her way, my dear."

Lottie nodded. She would do her best. But it was worrying to hear that someone like that had remembered her. Uncle Jack was still looking unusually grim, and he obviously didn't intend to discuss it.

"All I did was stop her from bewitching me," she told him pleadingly. "I don't know why she hates me so much."

Uncle Jack put his arm around her shoulders. "It's nothing to do with you, Lottie love. It all happened before you were born, or even thought of. Don't you worry."

What had all happened before she was born? Lottie thought. Sometimes Uncle Jack seemed to think she was about five. She wasn't supposed to worry? As if that was going to happen.

Sofie stretched, yawned, and stepped delicately off her cushion. "I feel *much* better," she announced. "Did

21

I miss anything? Are these mice exciting? Striped, perhaps?" She gave a dismissive sniff.

Giles bowed to her. "I am afraid I am not a mouse." He peered down at his stomach admiringly. "You could get about three mice out of me, I should think. Were you expecting mice? Am I in the wrong place?" He brushed his whiskers with one paw and looked apologetically at Uncle Jack.

"Well, possibly . . . My order was actually for some rather interesting Russian blue mice, but you are most welcome to stay. We specialize in mice, but I would be delighted to make the proper acquaintance of a hamster." Uncle Jack and Giles bowed to each other gravely, and Lottie began to think that the manners of everyone in the shop were about to undergo a serious improvement in order to live up to Giles's standards.

She left Uncle Jack and Giles exchanging polite small talk and beckoned Sofie to follow her upstairs. Sofie had lived with Uncle Jack for a while. He had bought her several years before as a present for his wife. Lottie thought Sofie had been rather lonely since her aunt died, which was why she'd been ready to be Lottie's familiar. Perhaps Sofie knew what Uncle Jack wasn't telling her.

"What is the matter?" Sofie asked as soon as they were curled up on Lottie's bed. Then she sniffed hopefully. "Wait a minute, do you have any chocolates left? I can smell truffles." She peered meaningfully at Lottie's bedside table.

Lottie got out the box and waited until Sofie was blissfully licking her lips in case she'd missed any. There was no point in talking to her while she was in the middle of a chocolate.

"Mmm. French chocolate. So obviously superior." Sofie opened her eyes at last and looked inquiringly at Lottie. "So. What is it, dear Lottie?"

"A horrible person's being horrible to her!" Fred popped his pink nose out of Lottie's school cardigan, making her jump. She'd forgotten he was there. "Have any chocolate for me too?" he asked hopefully.

Lottie sighed and handed over another truffle, plus another one for Sofie because she looked so mournful. It was probably a good thing that the animals ate so many — her mother tended to send her lots of chocolates and presents from Paris, because she felt guilty about being away. If Lottie ate them all she'd be the size of a house.

"What sort of horrible person?" Sofie asked at last.

"An enchantreth," Fred mumbled, his mouth smeared with chocolate. The chocolate was about the size of his head and he was making it last.

"I beg your pardon?" Sofie demanded frostily. She

liked to make her position as Lottie's familiar and confidante clear by bossing the mice around as much as possible.

"An enchantreth! Enchantreth! Bad witf! Oh, athk Lottie!" Fred took another nibble of chocolate.

"It was an enchantress," Lottie told her quietly.

Sofie blinked. "That one who came before?" she asked sharply, and Lottie nodded.

"Giles, that new hamster, met her while she was buying two dogs, salukis I think he said. Have you heard of those?" Lottie had no idea what salukis were like.

Sofie sat up very straight, almost as though she was trying to make herself look taller. "Nasty, rude dogs," she hissed.

"I've never heard of them. Where do they come from?" Lottie asked.

"Egypt," Sofie muttered huffily. "Oldest dogs in the world supposedly. Royal dogs of the pharaohs. *Nonsense.* Crazy as ferrets and too thin! Skinny!"

"Ohhhh." Lottie looked at Sofie, whose whiskers were positively vibrating with irritation. "Are they possibly quite . . . tall?"

"Maybe," Sofie spat. "Perhaps a little taller than me. But not much!" she added fiercely, glaring at Lottie.

"No, of course not," Lottie agreed. Sofie was so irritated that she wasn't controlling her thoughts, and a picture of a saluki was shimmering on Lottie's bedroom wall. It was a beautiful dog, a light creamy golden color, with long feathery fur and a pointed nose. It looked like a very aristocratic greyhound. It also looked completely insane, but Lottie was pretty sure that was only because it was Sofie's imagination that was in control. She could see why the saluki upset Sofie. It did have *very* long legs.

The saluki raced off into the distance, past Lottie's pink polka-dot curtains, and Sofie huffed angrily. "So, she got herself two crazy dogs. Huh."

Lottie looked at her thoughtfully. "Sofie, do you know anything about that enchantress that you haven't told me? Had you met her before? Uncle Jack knows her but he won't tell me why."

Sofie glanced up in surprise, the salukis forgotten at last. "No! He has not said. I had not seen her before she came to the shop that day — all I know is that she is evil. You could tell. She made the air taste bad."

"He said it all had to do with before I was born." Lottie looked around her bedroom, the pretty curtains, the polka-dot comforter, the pink fairy mirror. She wished she could remember more about her life at the shop when she was tiny. She had lived here with her parents when her dad and Uncle Jack ran the shop together. But after her dad died, her mum had left, too sad to stay and be reminded of him every day. She never understood the magic of the shop, and she knew nothing about Lottie's powers. Lottie wasn't sure she would ever be able to tell her — Mum just wasn't the kind of person who believed in magic.

Lottie sighed. She wished she knew more about her father too. He was a strange, shadowy figure in her life, only a memory from photographs. Lottie was never sure whether she really remembered those times or whether she'd simply imagined them from the few flat, bright pictures she had. Uncle Jack had given her a photo album with lots more pictures in it. She and Danny were playing in a kiddie pool while he and her father watched them, laughing. They looked so much alike. Lottie tried hard to remember, but she'd been a baby then. She tried to ask Danny if he remembered, but he denied it in disgust. He also said that if she ever let anyone see that photo he would pour molasses in her hair.

She couldn't help feeling closer to her father here, where he'd lived too. It was a place he'd loved. And Uncle Jack was his double, just a little grayer, as it was eight years since those photos had been taken. She wanted to know so much more about him. Uncle Jack didn't seem to want to tell her much. He would happily look at the photos with her and tell her what a sweet little girl she'd been, but if she started to ask about her father's magic or where he'd gone on that last trip, Uncle Jack would change the subject and then suddenly remember an urgent delivery he had to make. Lottie tried to remember that it had to be hard for Uncle Jack too — her dad was his brother, after all. But why did he have to be so secretive about him?

The last time her mother had come to visit, Lottie had forced her to tell more than she ever had before about her father. Lottie still felt the tiniest bit guilty because it had upset her mum to remember. But not that guilty. Her mum had refused to talk about her father for so long, Lottie figured she had a right to know.

Her mum was still angry. She hadn't wanted Lottie's dad to go on the trip to the rain forests and leave her and Lottie, and she'd thought he was crazy when he suggested they come too. Lottie found it hard to understand how they'd ever fallen in love and gotten married. They were so different! Mum was so sensible and cautious and desperate to look after Lottie by making sure she worked hard and earned enough. From everything everyone said, Lottie's dad wouldn't have cared where they lived and what they had to eat, as long as they were happy. Not to mention the fact that he had magic! How could Mum never have known? Lottie still found it impossible to believe. But then, Mum always had a sensible explanation for anything odd that happened. She was just like all the nonmagical people who came into the shop — their eyes seemed to slide over anything strange.

"I am sorry, Lottie," Sofie said gently, nosing at her arm. "I know you hate all this secrecy about your father. I promise you, I do not know what your uncle is hiding."

Lottie stroked her smooth head gently. "It's all right, I know." She closed her eyes for a moment and let Sofie's comforting furry thoughts fill her head. They were almost equally split between love of chocolate and love of Lottie.

"Shall we go downstairs?" Sofie suggested. "I would like to meet this hamster properly." Sofie felt it was her duty to interview any new arrivals at the shop. Lottie wondered if she and Giles would get along. They seemed equally strong-minded, and she could imagine them not being able to stand each other.

The stairs led right into the shop, and Lottie heard a familiar voice as they came down. Mr. Fieldfare was back, talking earnestly to Uncle Jack, while his friend Mr. Bucklebank wandered around the cages chirping to the mice.

"It's most peculiar," Mr. Fieldfare was saying worriedly. "Oh hello, Leah."

Uncle Jack raised his eyebrows, but Lottie made a "doesn't matter" face.

"Many of the artifacts she has in her windows are absolutely packed full of power. What if the wrong person bought them? It looks like one of those silly shops full of candles and crystals and getting your astrological chart drawn, whatever that is. But this stuff is far more dangerous. I just don't know what the owner can be thinking."

"It's definitely someone who knows what they've got?" Uncle Jack asked thoughtfully. "Not just a mistake? Someone who happened to collect all these things by chance?"

Mr. Fieldfare shook his head grimly. "No. It's a woman and she knows exactly what she's doing. Those windows are arranged to ensnare passersby. She wants control, Jack — I don't know why. For its own sake, maybe. This is a busy town. Hundreds of people pass by those windows every day. Even if only one stops — imagine the harm she could do them!"

Uncle Jack anxiously shook his head.

Mr. Bucklebank saw Lottie watching and smiled. "Someone has opened a magic shop," he told her in his low, musical voice. Lottie could imagine him bespelling people with a word — his voice thrummed with power. "Louis is most upset. He thinks it will upset the balance of everything in your pretty little town." He stroked a mouse's head gently with one finger and the mouse closed its eyes blissfully. "I'm not so sure."

"You think everything will be all right?" Lottie asked anxiously.

Mr. Bucklebank gazed down at her. He really was extremely tall. "No. Not necessarily. But sometimes the balance ought to be upset, don't you think? Life would be rather boring otherwise." He tickled the mouse under the chin and it fell over backward with its paws in the air, then struggled up, giggling. Sofie snorted with disgust. Mr. Bucklebank chuckled. "Balance, Lottie," he pointed out. "Sometimes it's quite fun to fall over."

Lottie looked at him doubtfully, but he was tickling the mouse again and he seemed to think their conversation was over. Lottie wasn't so sure about being unbalanced. As someone who would have laughed herself silly only a few months ago if anyone had told her she was going to live in a magic pet shop, she couldn't imagine what would happen if the whole town suddenly found out that magic was real. The only person she had told was Ruby, and that had been hard enough. She *trusted* Ruby. How would Zara and her gang react to the news?

"Lottie, don't worry." Uncle Jack was staring at her, looking concerned. "Do you remember what I said to you when you wanted to tell Ruby about the shop?" Uncle Jack asked her gently.

Lottie tried to think back, but eventually she shook her head apologetically.

"People have an amazing ability not to see things," Uncle Jack explained. "Like your mother."

"Oh yes." Lottie remembered now. "Only the right people would understand. But you said that Ruby might not want to be friends with me anymore," she added slowly.

"Exactly. She would always have felt that there was something strange about you, even if she couldn't quite put her finger on it. She wouldn't have trusted you." Uncle Jack sighed. "That's what Louis and I are worried about." He smiled sadly at her. "No, I've lived here so long. Our family belongs here. If people are suddenly suspicious about us, even if they don't know why, all that will be spoiled. This is my home. I don't want to leave."

"I don't want to either!" Lottie gasped. And it was true. Netherbridge felt more like home than the apartment where she'd lived with her mother. Sofie nudged her leg lovingly with a damp nose. Lottie had promised her that she would never go back there and leave her behind, but Sofie still couldn't help worrying about it. How could Lottie choose between Sofie and her own mother?

"If this new shop starts letting out all our secrets, life is going to be very difficult," Louis Fieldfare said grimly.

"Can't you stop it?" Lottie asked, looking back and forth between them anxiously.

Uncle Jack held out his hands in a despairing gesture. "How? We can't force this woman to close down. We have no power." He sighed. "Perhaps people just won't want to buy these things," he muttered.

Mr. Fieldfare gave a bitter laugh. "It may be dangerous magic, but it's disguised as love charms and fortune-telling. She'll be very busy." He sank glumly onto a stool by the counter.

"Cheer up, Louis." Mr. Bucklebank came in from the back room where he'd been admiring Uncle Jack's lizards. One of them was perched on his hat. "Tell Jack about your discovery."

Mr. Fieldfare smiled and shook his head. "Jacob thinks I'm imagining things, but I know I saw it. We went for a walk, the scenery here is so pretty, you know, and Jacob had never been to Netherbridge. And you'll never guess what we saw! A unicorn! Up on Netherbridge Hill, of all places."

Uncle Jack became pale. It was shocking to watch — all the color simply drained out of his face, leaving it white beneath his grizzled black hair.

"Oh! Oh, Jack, I'm sorry. I had forgotten." Mr. Fieldfare reached out and put a hand on his arm.

"Not in front of —" Uncle Jack waved a hand at Lottie, who was staring at them in amazement.

"No, no, of course not. No, indeed." Mr. Fieldfare stared at her.

"What is it?" Lottie begged, but Uncle Jack shook his head.

"Nothing. Nothing at all. An old memory, Lottie." He rubbed a hand over his face wearily. "Lottie, I need some fresh air. A quick walk. You and Sofie could mind the shop for me for half an hour, couldn't you? Danny should be home soon anyway."

Lottie nodded unwillingly. She knew he wouldn't tell her any more. Her uncle had an amazing ability to slide out from under questions. Danny had inherited it. Conversations with both of them could be like walking on shifting sand.

She watched as the three men hurried out of the shop. She was pretty certain where they were going.

Straight up to Netherbridge Hill.

Lottie got out her homework and sat at the counter staring at it, with Sofie on her lap. Giles the hamster was having a restorative nap in his new cage and had resolutely refused to wake up and be examined, even when Sofie gave him one of her best stares. This was impressive, as Sofie's stares could probably wake the dead. Sofie was very irritated and was taking it out on Lottie's homework by being very rude about her mock newspaper article.

The door clanged loudly and Lottie sat up. She put on a helpful smile and hoped whoever it was didn't actually want to buy anything because she hated using the cash register — it always bit her.

Sofie growled, a long, low whisper of a growl that woke every animal in the shop and put them on their guard immediately. It was a growl that meant *enemy*.

The mice buried themselves in their bedding with panicked squeaks, and even Selina and Sarafan watched nervously from their pen, tails twitching.

Lottie looked at the door hopefully. Surely Uncle Jack would be back soon? Hadn't it been almost half an hour? And where on earth was Danny when she needed him?

But there was no one there to help her. The white-haired enchantress in the red dress, the one who had some strange history with Lottie that she didn't understand, the one Giles had heard making odd threats, was now standing in front of the counter. Smiling.

"Lottie! How charming!" Her voice was like a peal of silvery bells, clear, sweet, insistent. Irresistible.

Lottie gulped and closed her eyes for a second, slamming shut all the doors in her mind.

The enchantress's smile showed more teeth. "That isn't very friendly, Lottie," she cooed. "Can't we talk, at least? You owe me that, don't you, after you shut me out of your mind so harshly when I was here last. That was rather rude, Lottie, dear. Not many people are rude to me. I can't quite decide what to do about you. Really, of course, I should just banish every thought you own so that you can never think again." Her voice was light and almost laughing, but it wasn't a joke.

She came closer and leaned against the counter, idly drawing circles on its dusty surface with a perfect fingernail. "But then, that might be a little shortsighted. There's something so interesting about a powerful new mind." She looked at Lottie for a moment, her head to one side, as though she was trying to decide on something terribly important, like which cake to have for dessert. Lottie had the awful feeling that the enchantress was crazy enough to think destroying her would be the same kind of decision.

Then she smiled suddenly, her eyes glinting. She seemed to be running down a different track now. "I'm your new neighbor, Lottie, did you know?" she asked. "I've bought a little shop just down the road. A little gift shop. I shall be keeping it much the same, with just the tiniest alterations in the stock here and there. Slightly *different* presents. I'm sure they'll have a most interesting effect. I should think that lots of your friends from school would enjoy a visit. Perhaps you could tell them about me?"

Lottie could feel the fear radiating from every animal in the shop. Sofie snuggled into her as close as she could go, her nose pressed into the crook of Lottie's elbow, trembling.

What is it about her that's so scary? Lottie wondered. *Why are we all so frightened?* Having the terrified thoughts of hundreds of tiny creatures in her head was making her feel worse than ever. She couldn't stop watching the enchantress's fingers, drawing those patterns on the dusty counter. Such a silly thing to do. Irritating, really. Lottie wished she'd stop. For some strange reason, the patterns were starting to make her feel dizzy.

"Ahem, ahem!"

Lottie blinked and shook the fuzzy feeling out of her head.

Giles the hamster marched across the counter (Lottie could almost hear the brass band thumping away inside her head, definitely a military tune) and took up a defensive position in front of her. He plopped his rather large bottom down and glared at the enchantress.

She laughed. "This little mouse is protecting you, Lottie dear! How perfectly sweet."

"I am not a mouse, madam," Giles replied icily. "I am a hamster. There are significant differences. Note the lack of a tail."

The enchantress raised her eyebrows slightly and stared at him. She clearly expected him to collapse into a quivering heap, but Giles just stared back. He was like a slightly grumpy little old man, Lottie thought, glaring at a bratty child. He seemed completely unafraid of the enchantress's magic.

She frowned and Lottie noticed how much less

beautiful it made her. Her face was so perfect, until it was spoiled by frown lines and a pouting mouth. She no longer looked as though she was made of some precious stone — she looked human and irritated. Suddenly she was much less frightening.

The enchantress raised a hand as though to point a spell at Giles. Lottie wasn't sure whether she would actually dare to do it. Last time she had been in the shop she'd clearly had a healthy respect for Uncle Jack, so harming one of his creatures might not be a wise move. But Lottie wasn't taking any chances. She snatched Giles up and held him close against her. Sofie growled a warning and all three of them stared at the enchantress.

"For future reference, Lottie, dear, mind the fur," Giles muttered.

"Sorry." Lottie could feel some of his unshakable confidence seeping into her fingers. She felt much better already.

The enchantress looked down at her fingers as though she thought something might be wrong with them. Lottie could almost hear her thinking, *Why can't I just squash them? A little girl and a fussy little dog and a hamster?*

We don't believe in her anymore, Lottie realized as she saw the mice creeping toward the bars of their cages curiously. *We don't believe she'll do all these awful things.* Then a sudden thought hit her and she gave a tiny gasp. *And that makes her all the more dangerous. Now she's got something to prove. She'll want us to go back to the way we were before. She's going to squish my mind!*

At that moment, the door clanged again and Uncle Jack walked in, looking considerably better than he had half an hour ago.

"You!" he snapped, his dark eyes flashing.

The enchantress wheeled around and backed against the counter.

"Get out of my shop, Pandora. Leave my niece alone."

"Your . . . niece." The enchantress blinked at him, clearly thinking fast.

"Yes. She's not mine. Is that what you thought? No. This is Tom's girl." Uncle Jack folded his arms, looking down at her almost triumphantly.

She bit her lip, staring at Lottie, her small white teeth actually cutting into the skin and leaving a tiny bead of blood. Then she plunged out of the shop, the door swinging closed behind her with a sigh.

Lottie slumped against the counter and Giles stepped out of her hands and strolled over toward Uncle Jack.

"More sunflower seeds, do you think, old chap?"

Lottie stood up, her legs shaking slightly. She was still hugging Sofie, grateful for the feel of soft fur under her fingers. She waited until Uncle Jack had finished pouring out a generous bowl of sunflower seeds for Giles, then she caught his eye as he glanced up. He looked at her, apologetic and rather embarrassed.

"I'm not going to get away with it this time, am I, Lottie?"

"Who *is* she?" Lottie demanded. "You know she's the one who bought the shop down the road, the one that Mr. Fieldfare was so upset about?"

"I did wonder," Uncle Jack admitted. "She's not going to be easy to get rid of." He sighed. "Her name is Pandora Gold. She's a witch. Just like Ariadne."

Lottie snorted. "No, she isn't. Ariadne said that before, that *she* could have been just like that, and it all depended on what you did. She was trying to warn me about not doing the wrong things with my magic.

There's no way Ariadne could be like that. That woman's evil!"

Uncle Jack nodded. "Absolutely. But she's made herself evil, Lottie. You don't get born a bad witch. You're made. Mostly by yourself." He paused. "Pandora turned . . . a few years ago. She was always a little too interested in controlling other people's minds, but she would at least convince herself that she had good reasons for it. She went away after that — she used to live in Netherbridge, you see — and I don't know what she's been doing the past few years. Stuff I'd rather not think about."

Lottie waited for him to say more, but he was watching Giles stuff his cheek pouches and carefully not looking at her. "Uncle Jack! What about the rest?"

Uncle Jack glanced up at her, blinked, and tried to look innocent. He only managed to appear shifty. He looked a lot like Danny. "The rest?"

"Why is she interested in me? She said it was because she couldn't get in my mind, but there's something else, isn't there? When you told her I wasn't your daughter, she looked like she'd swallowed a hedgehog. What is it? Tell me!"

Uncle Jack's eyes were full of hurt as he stared back at her. "I can't, Lottie. I promised. It isn't my story to tell."

"So who *will* tell me?" Lottie wailed.

Uncle Jack wandered away into the storeroom. "Only Pandora could tell you the whole story," he whispered bitterly. "The only other person who knows is dead."

Lottie went to bed early that night. Danny had finally gotten home from school late after soccer practice, which he hadn't told anyone he had. At least it cheered up Uncle Jack. He'd been worrying about how much Danny hated school, and knowing that Danny had joined a team made him feel much better. Septimus was less excited, or he pretended he was. When Danny could actually be bothered to do any magic, Septimus was his familiar and he adored Danny, even though he told him off constantly. He had to stay in the locker room during soccer practice, hiding in Danny's gym bag, and he complained about it bitterly. "The smell!" he moaned faintly to Sofie at the dinner table. "It's still on my fur. I may have to sleep on a lavender sachet tonight."

Sofie edged to the other side of her chair and continued delicately sucking spaghetti.

"I'm watching the game tonight, OK?" Danny told Lottie. "You can watch, too, if you like," he added graciously.

"I'd rather die," Lottie muttered. She was still edgy

from her encounter that afternoon and she didn't want to spend the evening with Danny lecturing her on soccer. "I think I preferred you when you hated everything. All this soccer stuff is really boring."

"You should get more exercise, Lottie," Danny told her pityingly, waving his fork at her. "Then you wouldn't be so moody. It's all to do with low energy levels, you know."

"If you watch this soccer game with him, I will never speak to you again," Sofie told Lottie, a string of spaghetti dangling from one side of her mouth. She slurped it up with a satisfying squelch and everyone shuddered. Considering she was a dog, Sofie normally ate very tidily, but spaghetti eating was not her strong suit.

Lottie climbed the stairs to her room with Sofie after dinner. She was planning to listen to some music and maybe read a bit. She'd asked Giles if he wanted to come, but he'd gracefully declined, saying that the afternoon had worn him out. When she passed his cage after dinner he was invisible under a pile of hay bedding that was very gently rising and falling with his snores.

Lottie sympathized. She was exhausted too. She turned her radio on and lay on her bed reading a magazine with Sofie beside her, but she kept dozing.

"If my boyfriend kept staring at other girls, I would bite him," Sofie suggested, reading the *"Love Letters"* page. She kept snorting disgustedly.

"Mmm. She should definitely dump him." Lottie yawned. "Oh, Sofie, I'm so sleepy. The enchantress — I know she's called Pandora but I still can't think of her as anything except the enchantress — she wore me out, I think. I felt like I was holding her out of my head the whole time she was here. She was like water trying to seep through the cracks."

"Me as well." Sofie nodded. "And the badness! She made me feel sick. She is no good, that one."

Lottie didn't answer. She had been leaning on her arms and staring at the magazine, but now her head had slipped sideways. Sofie nudged her gently so that she wouldn't get a crick in her neck and tugged the magazine out from under Lottie's cheek with her teeth. Then she burrowed herself lovingly under Lottie's arm and went to sleep too. Lottie felt her closeness and sighed softly in her sleep, wriggling until she was comfortable. They were warm and weary and safe.

Lottie stopped walking and looked back down over the little town. The path up Netherbridge Hill was steep and slippery, and it was nearly dark. The street-lights were just starting to come on below her and

Netherbridge looked cozy and welcoming, surrounded by hills, with the river snaking through and reflecting the amber lights in its dark water.

Lottie sighed, wishing they could go back home and drink hot chocolate with marshmallows in the shop with Uncle Jack. She even tried to take one or two steps back down the path, but she couldn't. They had to go on and find the unicorn. She knew it was important somehow, in that weird way one knows things in dreams. . . .

"Lottie, is this a dream?" Sofie demanded curiously.

"Oh! Yes, it must be." Lottie looked around her. Everything seemed very real. She had been up Netherbridge Hill once before, a few weeks ago, with Ruby. It had been a sunny weekend — they'd taken a picnic and lain on the sweet-smelling grass, gossiping about school.

Now it was chilly and the hills seemed steeper and craggier. Lottie shivered. It was getting darker every moment and a gusty wind was blowing. If there was a unicorn up here, there might be other things too. . . .

"Lottie, where are we going?" Sofie asked plaintively. "We have come a *very* long way."

Lottie gave her a surprised look. "The dream only started a minute ago. We've come about fifty yards, that's all!"

Sofie shook her head. "No, we walked all the way up, I am sure." She wrinkled her nose. "Well, it feels as if we have."

Lottie scooped her up, glad of her warm weight. The hill was very lonely and strangely quiet.

"Do you know where we are going?" Sofie asked again.

"Only that we're going to find a unicorn," Lottie told her, hoping she wouldn't start laughing.

"Oh! The one that Louis Fieldfare saw. He is a silly man, Lottie. He may have made it up. His unicorn might be no more than a rabbit with a white tummy."

"I know. But did you see the way Uncle Jack reacted when Mr. Fieldfare told him about it? It was like he got ten years older all of a sudden. He knows something about unicorns, Sofie. And Mr. Fieldfare knew about it, too — he remembered when Uncle Jack looked so ill. He was really sorry he'd said it. I was going to ask Uncle Jack about it, but then the enchantress came and she made me forget everything else."

"Mmm." Sofie looked thoughtful. "Dreams are good for remembering the important things. I do not know if unicorns are real, Lottie. I think they were once. But now — they may all be lost."

"Uncle Jack knew something about them. I'm positive he did." Lottie smiled excitedly. "After all, Sofie, Sam and Joe, Ruby's lizards, say that they're dragons and that their cousins are much bigger. So if dragons are real, why not unicorns?"

Sofie nodded consideringly. "Perhaps." Then her ears pricked up slightly, a sharper look coming into her eyes. "Lottie, can you hear something?"

"No-ooo, I don't think so." Lottie looked around anxiously. "Only the wind. Why, what can you hear?"

"Footsteps." Sofie peered grimly down the path behind them. "*Paws*. Large ones. Someone's coming, and they're trying not to let us hear."

"This is still only a dream, isn't it?" Lottie asked nervously. Being chased in the dark by something large with paws was making her think that it was actually more of a nightmare.

Sofie glanced up at her quickly. "I do not know. Dreams can be real too."

Lottie gulped. "Can we wake ourselves up?"

Sofie blinked. Then she shook her head. "No. Or at least, I cannot. Can you?"

Lottie shrugged helplessly. "No. Most of me thinks I already am awake. I don't know how." She shuddered. "Oh, Sofie, it's her, isn't it? Pandora?"

"Yes. And I think she has with her those dogs, the ones Giles told you about. They run very fast, Lottie. They do not ever stop until they have brought down their prey." Sofie was tense in Lottie's arms. "It would be better not to run," she admitted reluctantly.

"You mean we just have to stand here and wait for them to catch us?" Lottie gasped.

Sofie looked at her unhappily. "We cannot escape. And it is, perhaps, only a dream after all."

"It isn't," Lottie said grimly. "I can tell. She's down there, real as anything. What does she *want*? Oh, I wish Uncle Jack wasn't so cagey. Then at least we'd know what we are dealing with."

"Has Ariadne taught you anything that might help?" Sofie asked hopefully.

Lottie thought frantically. "Only those same closed-mind spells I used against Pandora before. I've done those really carefully. But mostly we've been working on finding my magic and keeping it under control. We've been practicing since you and I accidentally went into a trance and chased Zara's mind, that night after we first found our magic, when Fred and Peach had to bite me. Ariadne wanted me to know how to control the power and channel it, so we didn't get carried away."

"I think right now we should get carried away as much as possible," Sofie said grimly.

Lottie could hear them now. Scufflings and panting breaths, and an excited voice urging the dogs on in an angry whisper.

"Back up against the rock, Lottie," Sofie whispered. "We do not want those dogs behind us."

They flattened themselves against the rock wall that lined one side of the path. Lottie tried hard not to look scared. A lot of Pandora's magic was all show, she was sure. It was about telling people they were frightened so that they would be.

Pandora seemed to shine as she glided up the path. A soft yellow glow outlined her and she looked angelic.

"Tacky," Sofie muttered.

Lottie smiled. Thank goodness for Sofie. *She* had been thinking it was rather impressive and wondering how she could do anything against such strong magic. *Tacky* was a much more useful way to look at it.

Pacing on either side of the enchantress were two enormous dogs. They were very beautiful, one a golden brown color and one black. Their feathery fur shone in their mistress's magical light and they ran so gracefully that they seemed to float along beside her.

Sofie hissed angrily to herself and Lottie held her tightly. She could tell that Sofie was scared — she could feel Sofie's velvety-black fear pulsing in her own head. But Sofie was so proud that she might try to show that she wasn't frightened by leaping at one of the salukis. They might be beautiful, but their jaws looked fierce, and the two of them could probably have little Sofie for a light snack. Not that she would ever admit it.

The enchantress stopped an arm's length from Lottie and smiled kindly at her. It made Lottie's skin crawl. She stared back, forcing herself not to lower her eyes.

"Dearest Lottie," Pandora purred. "How lovely to meet you here. Such a happy coincidence. It's the most charming walk, isn't it? My favorite walk round here. I lived in Netherbridge before, you know, some years ago. I expect your uncle told you? About our . . . history?"

Lottie shook her head and Sofie whispered, "Coincidence!" in a disbelieving voice.

Pandora moved a step closer. "And even before I knew who you were, Lottie, I couldn't let a mind like yours get away. So rude, you know, to block someone out of your mind like that, the way you did when I first met you." She frowned for a moment. "But such power, Lottie. Such potential. A real waste that Ariadne is teaching you. I could do far more with a mind like yours than that feeble herb-gatherer. Do think about it. While you can." She smiled seductively, but her eyes were watchful. "No? Well, anyway, now that I am back among my old haunts, I love to exercise my dogs here. Prosper, Fatima, this is Lottie, with her own dear little dog. Lottie is a friend, so you are not to chase the poor little thing."

Lottie clutched Sofie in a death grip, knowing that she was desperate to leap for the enchantress's throat. Why was she being so horribly friendly now? Did she really want Lottie for an apprentice? Lottie felt like screaming, *I'm not your friend! I never want to learn anything from you!*

The salukis eyed Sofie watchfully. They looked hungry and twitchy, as though they would be delighted to chase down anyone who put so much as a foot out of place.

If we could wake up, now would be a very good time, Sofie said in her head.

I'm trying! Lottie promised her, but Pandora's cooing voice was wrapping around her, coating her mind in syrup. Uncle Jack loved to put maple syrup on pancakes, Lottie thought, smiling to herself. He would let Lottie mess around with the sweet-smelling bottle, trickling the syrup off a fork and letting it smooth itself out into a golden lake.

Syrup? Why on earth was she thinking about syrup? Her mind back under control, Lottie jumped, and screamed out loud. Pandora was right next to her, one hand on the rocky wall, the other reaching for Lottie's throat, and her face was like stone.

"This is a dream!" Lottie yelled, and smacked Pandora in the face as hard as she could.

The enchantress gasped, stepping back and putting a hand to her cheek in shock. But her shock didn't last long. The full force of Pandora's mind hit Lottie in seconds and it felt as if the rock wall had collapsed on her head.

Lottie whimpered, and worst of all, she could also hear Sofie whimpering in the darkness.

Lottie tried desperately to fight back, but Pandora was hammering at her thoughts and Lottie could feel that syrup seeping into the corners of her mind. Pandora was filling her head, forcing Lottie out.

Help me! she wailed, not sure whom she was crying to. She was watching the horrible, triumphant smile on the enchantress's face, miserably waiting for her to do whatever it was she was planning to do when she won. Was she going to steal Lottie's mind somehow?

Suddenly the smile faltered. Lottie blinked. What was happening?

What is that noise? Sofie hissed silently.

You're there! Lottie hugged her even tighter. She hadn't been able to feel Sofie since the enchantress had attacked.

Of course I am! Do not squeeze me like that. Something else is coming. And she is afraid of it. Look at her.

Lottie looked up at Pandora. She was gazing out at the hillside behind Lottie with an angry, frightened expression. The dogs were weaving around her nervously and she snapped at them.

At last Lottie heard it, what Sofie's sensitive ears had caught ages before. The thudding of hooves on the hard ground.

Lottie gasped. The unicorn! It had to be. She was so excited that she swung around to see, ignoring the enchantress entirely.

Galloping toward them was an enormous silver-white creature, his coat gleaming in the moonlight. He raced across the ground, making for the rocky wall behind Lottie and Sofie, and swung himself to a skidding stop on top of the crag, his hooves striking sparks from the stone. Then he put his head down, swung his enormous horn in between Lottie and Pandora, and growled, "Leave her."

"I shan't — you can't —" Pandora started to protest, but the unicorn's swiftly indrawn breath sent her stumbling backward.

"You will . . . *or else*," said the deep, snarling voice. It was frightening, that voice, but strangely familiar. It made Lottie feel safe. She couldn't help feeling that she must have met this unicorn before. But she couldn't have.

Pandora staggered away, her dogs glancing back fearfully, their tails hanging low as the unicorn watched them go.

Then he leaped gracefully down onto the narrow path, landing perfectly beside Lottie.

"Show-off," Sofie muttered. She wasn't grateful to be rescued.

The unicorn snorted with amusement and nudged her affectionately with his nose. "Take good care of her, little one," he whispered. Then he turned and galloped away up the path, a flash of white disappearing in the darkness.

Then Lottie woke up.

Lottie shivered, for the room was cold and dark now. She supposed Uncle Jack must have come to check on her and turned off her light. She sat up and Sofie wriggled into her arms. She was trembling too.

"Sofie, was — was that a dream? Or did it really happen? It seemed so real!" Lottie whispered shakily.

"It happened," Sofie muttered. "I don't know how she got us there, but she must have. She wanted to bind our minds, Lottie, to tie us to her. Make us hers. All that sweetness, that syrupiness — she was seeping in."

Lottie shuddered. "She asked if I wanted to be her apprentice. I think she was trying to make us hers somehow — whether we wanted it or not. I can't imagine anything worse."

"I do not want to think about it." Sofie shook her ears briskly.

"Where did that unicorn come from?" Lottie wondered. "He turned up just in time. I called out for someone to help, but I was hoping Uncle Jack or Ariadne or Danny would hear me somehow. I didn't expect a unicorn."

Sofie looked thoughtful. "It was not a unicorn."

"Sofie, it was! What else could it have been? It looked just like one! And it talked!" Lottie gazed at her, feeling almost hurt. Sofie had been there. How could she deny it now?

"It looked like a unicorn. But it was a dream creature, I am sure. Someone who loves you sent it to save you."

Lottie sat up. "Uncle Jack! It has to be. Like I said when we were in the dream, he looked awful when

Mr. Fieldfare mentioned unicorns. He must know something about them. I bet it was him." She got up, feeling her way carefully to the door. "There's still a light on downstairs, I can see it under the door. Let's go and find him."

They crept down the stairs to find Uncle Jack sitting at the counter, sucking his pencil and trying to work on the shop accounts.

"Lottie! Are you all right? Did you just wake up? I wasn't sure if I should wake you, but you looked so tired." Uncle Jack peered closer at her. "What's the matter? You look dreadful."

"Pandora chased us. She tried to bind us to her." Lottie slumped onto a stool next to him.

Uncle Jack put his pencil down and grabbed her arms. "What? I thought you were asleep upstairs!"

"We were. She was in my head. In my dream."

"Oh! You mean you had a nightmare." Uncle Jack sounded relieved.

"No!" Sofie yapped sharply.

Lottie shrugged. "Well . . . yes. I guess so. But it was real too. So it wasn't you then? I was sure it was," she muttered. "Especially after you got so upset about the unicorn before."

"What wasn't me? Lottie, you have to tell me what's

going on!" Uncle Jack was looking really worried again.

"We were up on Netherbridge Hill, in the dream, looking for a unicorn. Then Pandora turned up and she nearly got in my head, Uncle Jack, she was so strong. But a unicorn chased her away . . ." Lottie trailed off. It sounded so stupid.

"Like I said, Lottie, it was not a unicorn," Sofie said impatiently. "Somebody sent it to rescue us. It felt like you," she told Uncle Jack, in a considering tone.

"It wasn't," Uncle Jack said. "Listen, you two. There's something you need to know. Lottie, when your dad went off on that last trip, he wasn't just looking for exotic animals." Uncle Jack sighed. "He went to find unicorns, Lottie. He was obsessed with them and he'd heard rumors of unicorns somewhere in the deep rain forests. That's why I was so upset. Unicorns make me think of how much I miss Tom — and how much you've missed by not having him around."

"Oh," Lottie said quietly. She wasn't sure what to think. It was nice to know something more about her father, but at the same time, he'd abandoned her and her mum to go off chasing unicorns in a rain forest. Even though Lottie had seen one — or at least a dream one — unicorns still felt like a fairy tale. Something that a grown-up ought not to bother about. "I suppose we should go back to bed," she said wearily.

"Lottie!" Giles was looking down at her from the open door of his cage.

"Hi, Giles. Is your cage nice?" Lottie asked him, managing a small smile.

"Lottie, you can't go back to sleep," Giles told her urgently.

Lottie stared at him, then realized he was right, of course. "What if she comes back! What are we going to do?" Suddenly she was desperate to sleep, this minute.

"Ariadne will have to teach you a way to guard your mind while you're sleeping," Uncle Jack agreed. "But until then . . ."

"Until then, Lottie will have my cage in her room," Giles said calmly. "Hamsters are nocturnal. I shall be able to put in a spot of wheel running, keep myself trim. Any sign of a dream, enchantress or not, I shall jump on Lottie to wake her up." He smiled around at them modestly. "Do bear in mind that I am a trained battle hamster."

4

"I was so sure it was Uncle Jack," Lottie muttered sleepily.

"Does it matter who it was, Lottie?" Giles asked her kindly. His cage was perched on her bedside table and he was already working out on his wheel. "Someone cares enough to send a dream creature to rescue you. That's a good thing."

Lottie nodded. "Yes, but I still want to know who it was!" She thought for a moment. "Oh, of course! Sofie, we're being stupid — it must have been Ariadne. I'm just too tired to think. I'll ask her about it tomorrow. We can go after school."

Sofie curled up under Lottie's chin. "I would have thought that Ariadne would send a cat. Shadow or Tabitha. Not a unicorn."

"Maybe Shadow and Tabitha weren't big enough." Lottie yawned. "Go to sleep, Sofie. Good night, Giles."

Giles didn't bother to answer because Lottie was

asleep already. He scurried round and round on his wheel, guarding them as they slept.

Ariadne's shiny, polished kitchen, with all its modern gadgets, seemed the last place to be talking about unicorns, but she was fascinated.

"You really saw one? There have been rumors of a unicorn up there for a while." She sighed. "I know it was an awful experience, Lottie, but you *are* lucky. There are people who'd give all of their teeth to have been there with you."

"And their mother's," Tabitha put in, smirking.

Sofie yapped with frustration. "I keep saying this! It was not a unicorn! It was a dream creature!"

Shadow, who had been curled on Ariadne's lap, uncoiled himself and hissed, his near-blind eyes fixed on Sofie.

"Oh, do not be so bad-tempered," Sofie snapped. "Is no one allowed to disagree with your mistress? Pah."

"She knows a great more than you, little dog, about everything." Shadow's voice seemed to grow fainter every day, Lottie thought sadly.

"She does not because she was not there," Sofie retorted. "It was not a unicorn, it was a message that just looked like a unicorn."

"And if you didn't send it, either, who was it?" Lottie demanded.

"It may not have been a flesh-and-blood unicorn," Ariadne told Sofie, "but it must have come from someone who had met one. You can't send that sort of magical image without knowing what you're doing. Think about that thought image you made of Zara. You couldn't have done it if you didn't know her, could you? In fact, Lottie, you probably couldn't have done it without her sitting there just because you haven't had that much practice at this sort of thing."

Lottie nodded. Ariadne was right.

"I wonder if the person who sent the unicorn to you has done it before — perhaps sent out the dream image to see Netherbridge while they're somewhere else? That would explain the other sightings," Ariadne mused.

"Like *spying*?" Lottie asked in surprise.

Ariadne looked up. "Well . . . I suppose so. I hadn't thought of it like that."

"It could be very useful," Sofie added thoughtfully.

"Right now we need to concentrate on spells to close your mind while you're sleeping," Ariadne reminded them. "Close your eyes, Lottie."

*   *   *

The spells seemed to work — at least Lottie had no more strange dreams. But she couldn't help thinking that Pandora would not give up. She had been furious that Lottie had beaten her before, and knowing now that Lottie wasn't Uncle Jack's daughter apparently made it worse. Oh, if only Uncle Jack would tell her what was really going on!

Lottie had to walk past Pandora's shop every morning. She could have gone the other way, up the street and along for a while, but that was stupid. She wouldn't let anyone see that she was scared. The shop was horrible. Even Lottie, who knew hardly anything about magical artifacts, could see that this stuff was dangerous. In between the pretty china figures and the beaded jewelry were odd things. Not obviously bad, just strange. But Lottie could see the deceptive magic tied to them. That funny little toy velvet cat, for example. Its bead eyes were definitely following her down the street every morning and she could hear its giggly purr in her head. *Buy me! Buy me! We'll have so much fun!* She hated to think what Pandora might have enchanted it to do.

She sped past this morning, trying not to look in the window. But a sudden movement behind the glass caught her eye and she glanced up without meaning to. Inside the shop, Pandora wiggled her fingers in a teasing little wave. Lottie flushed scarlet. Pandora had been watching for her, had probably seen her avoid looking at the shop. She'd planned this and Lottie had done exactly what she wanted.

Made you look! The little velvet cat purred with delight and Lottie shuddered, racing off down the street.

Obviously Pandora hadn't given up. Lottie had to be on her guard all the time. At least she was pretty sure that Pandora couldn't get her at school. Not that she needed to. Zara Martin still did her best to make Lottie's life miserable the whole time she was there. She had discovered Pandora's shop already, which Lottie felt was just typical. She should have expected it, she supposed. Zara lived to shop and was always boasting about her shopping trips and the amount of money she'd made her mother spend.

A couple of days ago she'd been flaunting a little china doll at school. It was beautiful, with fair skin, blue eyes, and dark hair — it looked exactly like Zara, spookily enough. The eyes moved, Lottie was prepared to swear to it. Zara was showing the doll off at lunch and she'd shown it to Ruby. It had been almost as though she didn't want to, however. As though the doll had made her do it. There had been a puzzled expression in Zara's eyes as she muttered, "Ruby, have you

63

seen this?" and her hands had moved jerkily as she held it out.

Ruby had reached over to touch the doll's silken hair almost in a trance and Lottie had pulled her back, suddenly scared, but not fast enough to stop her. Just a split-second's touch couldn't have hurt her, could it? Lottie was almost sure it couldn't, but it bothered her. She shuddered to think how many other people in Netherbridge had already bought things from Pandora's shop.

The woman in the candy shop had been really strange with her when she popped in to get some peanut brittle for Giles and the pink mice yesterday. Usually she was friendly, but she'd snapped at Lottie, telling her to stop hanging around the candy and that she shouldn't think she was getting away with stealing anything. She'd been twirling an odd glass necklace around and around her finger as she said it. Lottie couldn't blame everything that went wrong on Pandora (much as she'd like to), but the necklace looked a lot like one of the ones in Pandora's window.

Lottie dashed onto the bridge and looked around for Ruby. But she wasn't there. Ruby was almost always there waiting for her, and Lottie wasn't particularly early today. She looked at her watch — in fact, she was almost late. Ruby had better hurry up. It was at least ten minutes' walk to school from here, and that was all they had.

Five minutes later, Lottie gave up and started to run. Perhaps Ruby was ill? But surely she'd have called the shop and said so? Ruby's mum knew they walked together — she would have called, even if Ruby was too ill to do it. Feeling grumpy, Lottie dashed into school five minutes late and skidded into her seat just as Mrs. Laurence started to take attendance. Her teacher frowned disapprovingly, and Lottie tried to look apologetic. She was having a hard time not looking furious. Ruby was in her usual place, right next to Lottie. From the look of her side of the table — pens neatly laid out, a doodle already started in her student planner — she'd been there a while.

"Where were you?" Lottie whispered angrily.

Ruby blinked and looked confused. "What do you mean?"

"Why weren't you waiting for me at the bridge?" Lottie sounded hurt. How could Ruby have forgotten? But she was acting as though that was exactly what she'd done.

Ruby flushed pink, her freckles merging with the blush. "Oh, Lottie, I'm really sorry! I don't understand.

That was so stupid. I just walked on my own like I used to. I'm sorry. Did you wait for me?"

"Of course I did, and now Mrs. Laurence's really irritated!"

Luckily, Mrs. Laurence didn't stay angry with Lottie, but the morning was still miserable. Lottie felt really hurt that Ruby had forgotten her, and Ruby was strange all day. Several times she seemed not to hear when Lottie said something, and at lunch she started to walk to a table at the other end of the cafeteria from where they usually sat.

"Ruby? Ruby! Where are you going?" Lottie tried to chase after her, nearly losing the plate of pasta from her tray.

Ruby looked around vaguely, then her face cleared. "Oh sorry, Lottie, I wasn't thinking." And she headed back to their normal table.

By the end of the day, Lottie almost felt like she wasn't there. Ruby just seemed to keep forgetting about her. She didn't think Ruby was doing it on purpose — she seemed so surprised and apologetic every time she did it. But Lottie just couldn't believe the way she was behaving. She hadn't even had a chance to tell Ruby about Pandora in the shop this morning.

"So are you planning on walking back home with

me today?" Lottie asked as they put their coats on. She felt a bit mean saying it, but she was upset. Maybe Ruby ought to see how she felt.

Ruby gave her a surprised look. "Oh OK. Sure." And she walked out, swinging her bag over her shoulder.

Lottie stared after her, tears actually stinging her eyes. Ruby hadn't intended to walk with her at all. She'd forgotten her again. This was awful. She followed a few steps behind Ruby, feeling embarrassed. She didn't want to be there if she wasn't wanted. She felt as though she was getting on Ruby's nerves, being too friendly. Maybe Ruby just didn't like her anymore. She was too nice to say it outright, so she was just trying to back off from Lottie and make it obvious that way. Lottie hadn't felt this depressed since her mum had dumped her and rushed off to Paris — that was how it had felt at the time anyway.

"Are you coming then?" Ruby called, turning around and walking backward to look at Lottie. She didn't sound that bothered either way. Lottie half wanted to yell back that no, she wasn't, thanks very much, but she hated the thought of walking home on her own. She scurried after Ruby, desperately trying to think of something to say — to Ruby, her best friend, to whom she could usually say whatever she liked.

They'd had a whole conversation last week when they just said the names of songs, and it was silly and weird and great. Now Ruby felt like a stranger.

Ruby sometimes popped into the pet shop on the way home from school with Lottie. It was out of her way, but her mum didn't mind as long as she wasn't too late getting home. Lottie asked, trying to sound offhand about it, "You coming to the shop?"

"Mmmm." Ruby shrugged. And then they didn't say anything else for ages.

They were just walking into Lottie's road when Ruby suddenly brightened. "Oh, there's that new shop. I really want to get something for my mum for her birthday. They might have something a bit different. I'm just going to pop in there now."

"No!" Lottie gasped in horror. She really didn't want Pandora to meet Ruby. She had the most definite feeling about it.

"Why not?" Ruby asked blankly, staring at her. "Whatever's the matter with you, Lottie? You're being so weird today."

"Me?" Lottie whispered, watching miserably as Ruby pushed open the shop door. The doorbell rang with a sickeningly sweet chime. Lottie wanted desperately to run home, but she couldn't leave Ruby there. She slunk after her, coughing a little as the door closed behind her. Even the perfumed air of the shop seemed poisonous.

It was an eerie place. Lottie had gotten used to the way that, when someone entered the pet shop, all the animals seemed to pause and hold their breath while they decided whether they could keep talking or not. But she hadn't been expecting it to be the same here. A display of unpleasant-looking string puppets hanging on one wall had obviously stopped moving just as the bell rang. Lottie wondered if Ruby would notice that their arms and legs weren't floppy like they should be. Their painted eyes flicked from side to side as the girls moved into the shop, and a nasty-sounding whispering came from their scarlet-painted mouths.

That one. She knows. The other's an innocent. Don't move!

Was everything in the shop magical? She couldn't exactly tell. Even the pretty china figurines that had belonged to the old lady who owned the shop before looked different now. Their sweet faces seemed too pretty, and their eyes were knowing.

There were some stranger things buried among the gifts, odd musical instruments, carved wooden whistles, and sets of pipes. Lottie wondered what they would sound like if she blew them, and shuddered.

Pandora was sitting behind the counter reading a

little black-covered book. It looked unpleasant, as though it might be full of dark secrets.

"Lottie!" Pandora cooed. "And you've brought a friend. How lovely."

Ruby looked around in surprise. "You know her?" she whispered.

Lottie opened her mouth but Pandora spoke first. "You might say we're old family friends," she said smoothly.

Lottie stared at her with dislike, but Pandora smiled back, seemingly amused.

"I'm looking for a birthday present for my mum," Ruby explained.

Pandora got up. "How nice. And did you have anything particular in mind?"

Ruby shook her head. "No, not really. She's quite hard to buy for. She likes unusual things. She's an artist."

"Oh, you've definitely come to the right place, Ruby." Pandora clapped her hands. "We have lots of unusual things."

Ruby blinked and stared at Pandora. "How did you know my name?"

"Well, you're a friend of Lottie's. I know an awful lot about Lottie, you see. And friends are so very, very important, wouldn't you agree?"

"I suppose . . ." Ruby faltered, but Pandora wasn't looking at Ruby. She was staring at Lottie, her eyes like flint.

Lottie glared back. She was angry now. How dare the enchantress threaten her friends? Lottie looked over at Ruby, who was admiring some stone eggs in a bowl, and her heart jumped with fear. Not fear for herself but fear for Ruby. And guilt. Was she putting Ruby in danger by being friends with her? What if Pandora tried to do something to Ruby just to hurt Lottie? It seemed so unfair that Ruby should be dragged in when it didn't have anything to do with her.

Then Lottie had a horrible thought. What if Pandora already had? She'd been thinking all day that Ruby had been acting weird and not like herself. They'd been best friends yesterday, and today she was behaving like she hardly knew Lottie. Ruby wasn't the kind of person to bottle things up. If something Lottie had done had upset her, she'd say so. So why the sudden change?

It was as if someone had put a spell on her. . . . The doll! Ruby had touched the doll! Could it really have enchanted her? Just that quick touch? It seemed unlikely, but Lottie was sure the doll had something to do with this.

That's what Pandora's heavy hints were about. She'd bewitched Ruby, and she wanted Lottie to know about it. Lottie looked up again and met Pandora's eyes, staring at her grimly. *I'll fight*, she whispered in her head, knowing that Pandora could hear. *You won't get her. I'll fight for her.*

Pandora smiled. *I know.*

5

Lottie went back to the pet shop alone, feeling shaken. Ruby seemed to have forgotten she was supposed to be going to Lottie's house. As they left Pandora's shop, she just turned the other way without even saying good-bye.

Ruby hadn't bought anything for her mother. She said she needed to try feeling out her mum for what she wanted — but she'd bought a black felt cat for herself. As Ruby walked up the road, Lottie could see it sticking out of the pocket of her backpack, grinning at her.

"What is wrong?" Sofie demanded as Lottie walked in, trailing her backpack. "You look like you have seen a ghost. And there are no ghosts on this street, or I would have smelled them," she added matter-of-factly. "Not the unicorn again?"

Uncle Jack was selling sugar mice to Mrs. Higgins for her two spoiled and bossy Siamese. He glanced worriedly over at Lottie, and his customer smiled at her. "Bad day at school, Lottie?" she asked. "At least it's the weekend, dear. I'll bring you some of my special tea next time I'm in. That'll perk you right up."

Lottie managed to say something polite back, and Mrs. Higgins dropped the sugar mice into her enormous shopping basket on wheels. A dark paw reached out to claim them. She pinched Lottie's cheek as she left and murmured something about the poor motherless dear, which usually would have had Lottie fuming, but right now she just didn't care.

"Don't ever drink her 'tea,' Lottie," Uncle Jack warned. "Lethal stuff. Turns your pee blue," he added in a whisper.

Lottie blinked at him, and he stared at her in concern. "Not even a tiny giggle? What's up, Lottie?" Then his face hardened. "It's Pandora, isn't it? What's she done now? She didn't try and get in your head again? Did Ariadne's spells work?"

Lottie shook her head. "She's cleverer than that. She went for Ruby instead. Ruby's hardly talking to me, and she wanted to go in Pandora's shop. She bought this evil little black toy cat. I don't know what to do. It's almost like she can't see me. She's not going to listen if I try to tell her what Pandora really is."

Uncle Jack frowned, and Sofie nuzzled Lottie's ankles comfortingly. "Ruby will come around," she said, her voice only slightly doubtful. "Pandora will not deceive her for long."

Lottie looked down at her. "No, you don't understand. Pandora's bewitched her, Sofie. She must have done."

"It does sound like it." Uncle Jack sighed.

"What can we do?" Lottie asked. "How do you break a spell?"

"It is not easy." Sofie shook her ears. "Not easy at all."

"You need some idea of how it's been cast," Uncle Jack explained. "Pandora probably discovered Ruby when she was in your mind the other night."

"She hinted something like that," Lottie admitted. "I'm pretty sure she got Ruby to touch a doll from her shop. Zara had it at school. The thing is, Ruby didn't start being odd until today. She was just like herself yesterday, even after she'd touched the doll. So I don't think that was the whole spell. Maybe Pandora was just using it to get a feel for Ruby. Does that make sense? To find her so she could do the spell? I've no idea how she actually cast it, though. How do I find something like that out?"

Sofie and Uncle Jack exchanged glances, and Sofie shrugged expressively. "You cannot. Unless you go into her mind."

Lottie glared at them. "Are you crazy? Is that the best suggestion you've got? She'd make mincemeat of me!"

"You underestimate yourself, Lottie, always," Sofie told her quietly.

"No point in sending untrained troops into battle," a squeaky voice pointed out from the wobbling mound of straw bedding in Giles's cage. He was back to sleeping in the shop now that Lottie had learned the guarding spells to ward off Pandora while she was asleep. Eventually he lumbered out of his nest and came toward the cage bars. "Lottie has the talent, to be sure, but she needs training! Drills! Discipline!"

"You sound just like Ariadne." Lottie sighed.

Giles marched up and down his cage lecturing them like a commanding officer. "To meet the enemy, one must be prepared! Mentally! Physically! Psychologologologically!" He paused there and coughed, as though he suspected he'd gotten that slightly wrong. "Emotionally as well," he added, combing his whiskers with an embarrassed paw.

"Because one day I think Lottie will have to fight her." Sofie's ears drooped. Evidently she was as worried about this as Lottie was.

The tense silence was broken by the clang of the shop bell, and the door swung slowly open.

"What the . . ." Uncle Jack peered around. The door seemed to have opened by itself. Little scratchy, scurrying footsteps pattered in, and everyone looked at the floor.

Staring up at them were two large and beautiful blue lizards, both looking rather bluer than usual. Lottie gazed down at them in surprise — they were unmistakable. Ruby's pets, Sam and Joe.

"For pity's sake, a space heater," Joe gasped.

"Hair dryer, hot water bottle, anything!" Sam added. "It's icy out there!"

Lottie gave them a surprised look. It was a nice crisp October day, not particularly cold. But Sam and Joe were cold-blooded and lived in a heated tank in Ruby's bedroom. Probably it did feel freezing to them.

Uncle Jack was fussing around, putting on the kettle and trying to remember where Grandma Maisie's old electric blanket was, while the lizards shivered and grumbled.

"Above and beyond the call of duty, Lottie, that's what this is," Sam growled.

"Duty has no higher limit," Giles pronounced disapprovingly.

Sam and Joe turned their disconcerting reptilian glare on him, but he didn't seem to mind. All the mice had hidden themselves under their bedding — they hated lizards. But Giles merely stared back, looking unimpressed. "To do one's duty is the highest calling of any creature," Giles said loftily. "Even reptiles," he added.

Uncle Jack reappeared with two hot water bottles, and the lizards surged onto them with moans of relief. "Aaahhh, that's better. My scales felt like they were falling off," Sam said gratefully. "What is that creature over there?" he asked Uncle Jack quietly as he put a blanket over his tail.

"A hamster," Uncle Jack explained.

"Ah. Fierce?"

"Extremely."

"Um-hm." Sam gave Giles a thoughtful look. "Quite small. No more than a few mouthfuls."

"Large teeth though," Joe muttered. "Crazy eyes, too, if you ask me."

"Why are you two here?" Lottie asked, thinking it might be a good time to interrupt.

Sam and Joe exchanged a worried glance. "It's Ruby," Sam explained.

Joe leaned forward and hissed impressively, "She forgot to feed us!"

"She's *never* done that before," Sam said sorrowfully.

"Oh my goodness, I'll get you some food at once." Uncle Jack was horrified. He adored lizards, and Sam and Joe were particularly rare and interesting. They were, according to them anyway, dragons. But Lottie wasn't sure if that was just wishful thinking. Their one aim was to breathe fire, and they were convinced they would do it someday.

Uncle Jack found a sack of his homemade lizard treats, squashy black lumps that were made out of mashed-up things Lottie didn't want to know about. But they did at least mean the pet shop never had any spiders. Sam and Joe gorged themselves, managing three each before they collapsed on the counter, burping gently.

"Is that better?" Uncle Jack asked anxiously. "You must have been starving."

Sam smiled sleepily at him. "Well, no. Ruby didn't feed us, but we're quite capable of opening the food box."

"But it was very nice of you to worry," Joe told him kindly.

Uncle Jack made a face and moved the rest of the treats out of reach. "Just don't be sick!"

Sam gave one last enormous burp and sat up, looking businesslike. "What's important is that Ruby is not herself."

"Definitely not," Joe agreed. "She's hardly looked at us the last couple of days."

"Except that odd moment last night," Sam added. "She was dreaming, I think. Wriggling about in her sleep. Then she got up and came and stood, leaning against the glass of our tank. Her face was white and her eyes were strange. She was still asleep, maybe. She stood there for ages, muttering, saying that she didn't understand and she couldn't think."

"She's been bewitched." Joe nodded importantly. "We need you to rescue her."

Lottie nodded. "Yes, we think the same thing. But we don't know how to break the spell. You two could look for clues, though, couldn't you? Something to tell us how Pandora cast the spell in the first place."

"Pandora? You mean you know who did it?" Sam looked up at her sharply.

Lottie hung her head, feeling ashamed that she was letting her friend down. "Yes, but it doesn't help. We don't know how to stop her."

Sam and Joe stared at her, their round black eyes hard. Eventually they seemed to decide she was telling the truth. "We'll go back and look," they agreed. "We'll watch her. She may let something slip."

"How did you get here though?" Lottie asked suddenly.

"We walked," Joe said bitterly.

"And no one saw you?" Uncle Jack asked in surprise. "You were lucky."

"I'll carry you back in my backpack," Lottie suggested. "Uncle Jack, is there any way Sam and Joe can let us know if they find a clue without having to come back again?"

"If you let us, we can speak in your thoughts," Sam suggested. "We would have done that this time, but you've got a thick wall up."

"Oh!" Lottie hadn't realized that the lizards could talk telepathically. "Usually only Sofie does that. And Tabitha and Shadow, I suppose." The unicorn had spoken in her mind, too, but as that night was becoming only a memory, Lottie was slowly beginning to wonder if she'd imagined him after all.

Uncle Jack smiled. "Most creatures can if you let them, Lottie. But at the moment, I think you're wise to be cautious. Just let your guard down for a minute, so Sam and Joe can feel your mind."

It was hard to relax the defenses she had built up so carefully. Lottie closed her eyes and stilled her breathing, seeking out the lizards. She'd never felt for them before, and their minds were slow and different and strange.

We'll find you again, Lottie.

Yes, we'll find you when we need you, Sam told her approvingly. *Good girl.*

Lottie blinked, and then opened her eyes. It felt odd looking at the bright paint of the shop and the glittering metal of the cages. Even the lizards' blue scales seemed glaring. Their thoughts had been quiet and softly tinted, and the rest of the world seemed too loud.

"I'll take you back home," she said, tipping her books out of her backpack. "Sofie, do you want to take a walk?"

Sofie uncurled herself luxuriously. "Not really, but I will come. You do not want Ruby to see you out near her house without an excuse."

Lottie flushed slightly. Of course Sofie knew what she was thinking, but she did sometimes wish that the little dachshund wouldn't *tell* everybody.

"Lottie, wake up! The sun is shining. I want to go out!"

Lottie groaned. Sofie was rarely energetic, but she could be an unstoppable force when she felt like it. She adored the sun, and she'd missed it these last few misty days.

"We must go to the park!" Sofie said, stomping her front paws up and down on Lottie's stomach so there was absolutely no chance of her going back to sleep.

"Now?" Lottie asked feebly. "On a Saturday? Before breakfast?"

"Oh well, no . . ." Sofie jumped off the bed. "Of course not before breakfast. I will have a croissant. Come *on*, Lottie!"

Lottie staggered out of bed and got dressed, then headed downstairs to find Sofie already sipping delicately from a bowl of black coffee. Uncle Jack was warming croissants. Lottie poured herself some orange juice and tried to stay awake. She'd dreamed about Pandora's shop all night, it felt like, seeing odd, mean little faces peeking out at her from the glass ornaments. The worst thing was, she'd seen Ruby reflected in them too.

Lottie pushed away her juice. She couldn't taste it properly anyway.

"Walk!" Sofie said briskly, watching her. "You will feel better. I shall fetch my leash."

Sofie was right. It was a gorgeous autumn day, and Lottie did feel better watching Sofie jump through the piles of orangey-brown leaves gathered by the side of the road. She sank into them almost to chin height and bounded along, ears flapping wildly.

"Was that extra-strong coffee?" Lottie muttered, but Sofie just shook her ears happily.

They weren't the only ones in the park. Lots of people

from Lottie's school were hanging around, the boys mostly throwing leaves at one another or playing soccer. It was one of the things that Lottie loved about Netherbridge — the town was so quiet and safe that parents let their children do far more things on their own than she'd ever been allowed to do at home.

"Look, there's Zara!" The fur along Sofie's spine was sticking up a little, and her ears were pricked watchfully. Lottie glanced over, trying to be casual. She still didn't want to get into anything with Zara, even if she wasn't as scared of her as she used to be.

Zara's little gang was sitting around the edge of the marble fountain, which had been turned off at the end of the summer. They were gossiping and giggling, and Zara's chief confidante, Bethany, had just pointed Lottie out.

"Ignore them," Sofie said, prancing on and jumping at a falling leaf. "Look, Danny is over there, playing soccer. And there is Ruby, too, under that tree."

Lottie caught her breath anxiously. She'd almost called Ruby this morning after all those bad dreams, but Ruby's strange behavior the day before had put her off. What if Ruby wouldn't talk to her? Lottie couldn't bear to hear her best friend tell her to go away. Ruby had helped her to settle in in Netherbridge. Lottie needed her. And she was pretty sure that Ruby needed her, too, especially now.

Telling herself not to be so silly and that maybe Ruby had just been having a bad day, Lottie strolled over to her. "Hey!" she said, a little hesitantly. "Are you OK?"

She'd been hoping that Ruby would be back to her old self, full of their plans for tonight — their Halloween night in with popcorn and a chick flick with strictly no monsters, ghosts, or evil twins. But Ruby looked up at her blankly and Lottie's heart sank. She was the same as before, maybe worse. It was as though she wasn't sure who Lottie was. She smiled politely, but her face brightened when she saw Sofie. She crouched down to stroke her ears.

Sofie looked up at Lottie thoughtfully. Lottie shrugged. She knew what Sofie was asking — whether she could talk to Ruby now. She had before, of course, but now they weren't sure whose side Ruby was on, or how she'd react to a talking dog. In the middle of a park full of people wasn't the place to find out.

But it seemed that stroking Sofie was bringing Ruby back to her senses. Perhaps Sofie's magic, which was so linked to Lottie's, was working against Pandora's spell. Ruby stopped petting Sofie's ears and looked at her in confusion. "What *are* you?" she murmured, drawing her hand back and staring at it.

Sofie opened her big dark eyes wide and fluttered her eyelashes, trying to look as innocent as possible. She overdid it slightly.

Ruby stood up, blinking, and backed away, glaring suspiciously at Lottie. "Are you making fun of me?" she asked angrily. "Teaching your dog to do tricks — it's . . . it's not nice!"

Lottie caught her breath, not sure what to say. She obviously couldn't tell Ruby that she hadn't taught Sofie anything, that in fact it was the other way around. "She didn't mean to," Lottie muttered, knowing it sounded stupid.

"I hate you!" Ruby snapped, her blue eyes sparkling furiously and her dark red curls escaping from under her hat like angry snakes.

It was no comfort to Lottie to know that this was all due to Pandora's spell. Tears burned at the back of her eyes. "You don't! No, you don't!" she whispered miserably.

"Ooh, look! Lottie and Ruby are having a little fight!" someone jeered, and Lottie spun around in horror. Zara, of course. She'd forgotten that the gang was there by the fountain. They had an amazing nose for trouble.

"Lottie's *crying*." Bethany laughed.

Lottie sniffed defiantly. "No, I'm not," she snapped. "And it's none of your business what Ruby and I are talking about, Bethany. Get lost."

"Does *Ruby* want us to get lost?" Zara asked silkily. She was an expert at divide and conquer. "Maybe you're being mean to her. I'm not sure we should leave her alone with you. Especially not with that vicious little dog around."

"You're more vicious than she is!" Lottie cried. "Ruby, I know you're upset with me, but this is *Zara*! Come on! Tell her to leave us alone. Please!"

Ruby was turning her head from side to side, looking confused and angry. "Why don't *you* leave me alone, Lottie," she snapped. "Don't boss me around. I'll talk to who I want, and right now I don't want to talk to you!"

"Go Ruby, go Ruby!" Zara and her friends chanted like cheerleaders, egging them on.

Ruby smiled slightly. She still looked confused, but it was obviously easier to accept Zara's support than to figure out what was going on here. She stepped closer to Lottie and hissed, "Just get lost!"

It was a mistake to come so close. Lottie's misery boiled over into anger, and she snapped back. "Fine! Go off and play with your new *friends* if you've forgotten what they're really like! I just hope you don't regret it, that's all!"

Sofie growled angrily, and Ruby hissed at her too. "Horrible little dog! I could step on you!"

Lottie and Sofie lost their temper together. Lottie shoved Ruby and Sofie bit her. It wasn't a very hard bite because she had to make a flying leap to get above Ruby's red leather boots, but she tore Ruby's tights just below the knee, and her teeth grazed the skin. Half triumphant, half shocked at what they'd done, Lottie scooped up Sofie protectively in case Ruby tried anything.

She didn't. She stood there looking down at the slowly bleeding scratch as though she didn't know how she'd gotten it. She didn't even say anything. It was left to Zara and the others to screech about vicious dogs and calling the police.

At last Ruby looked up and stared Lottie right in the face. She didn't seem confused anymore. She was frightened, and Lottie had an awful feeling that she was frightened of herself. Ruby's blue eyes held hers with a pleading expression.

"Lottie — help me!"

6

Zara had hustled Ruby away, but Lottie hadn't tried to stop them. The mist had closed down over Ruby's eyes again after she'd begged for help. It seemed that the pain of Sofie's bite had jolted her awake just long enough. Now the spell had swallowed her up again.

Lottie started to trudge home, carrying Sofie. At least she now knew for certain that Ruby was under a spell, and it wasn't that her friend didn't like her anymore. But she'd been pretty sure about that, anyway, except in her most doubtful moments. What she still didn't know was what on earth she was going to do about it.

Running footsteps thudding over the grass behind her made her turn quickly, thinking that it might be Zara and the others. She sighed gratefully when she realized it was only Danny.

"What happened?" he gasped. "I was on the other side of the field, and I couldn't see very well. Jake said he saw Sofie bite Ruby!"

"I was provoked," Sofie muttered sulkily.

"You didn't?" Danny asked in dismay.

"I might have . . ." Sofie spoke to the air over Lottie's shoulder to avoid looking at Danny. She knew quite well that biting wasn't allowed.

"She did. But Ruby was being really mean. And it was a good thing," Lottie promised him. "It brought Ruby out of the spell for a minute. She asked us to help her."

"Anyway, Lottie pushed her first," Sofie added.

"Wow," Danny muttered. "I wish I'd been there."

"You don't," Lottie said sadly. "It was awful. She was being so nasty, and then when she asked us for help she just looked really confused. Like she didn't know what was going on inside her." She sniffed. "You won't tell your dad, will you?"

Danny glared at her. "Oh yes, because I'm going to go straight home and say, *Da-ad, Lottie shoved her frie-ennnnd*. Honestly, Lottie, what do you think I am? A girl?"

"I'll shove you next," Lottie muttered. But he did cheer her up a bit.

"There has to be a way of breaking Ruby out of that spell for good," Danny said thoughtfully as they turned into their road. "Hey, cross over, Lottie. I'm not walking past that shop; it gives me the creeps."

Lottie gave him a surprised look.

"What? It's horrible!" exclaimed Danny. "Have you been making yourself walk right past the windows?"

"I went *in* it with Ruby," Lottie admitted.

"You're crazy. There's no point in giving her a golden opportunity to mess with your head twice a day, Lottie. Those windows are really strong. Pick your battles. Hey, that reminds me. We'll get Giles and ask him to help us break the spell. Sep's been talking to him, and he says he's got some great ideas."

"He was amazing when Pandora came into the shop," Lottie agreed. "He wasn't scared of her at all."

"I did tell you he was also utterly insane." Septimus's head popped out from the pocket of Danny's fleece. "There's brave and then there's just stupid."

They woke Giles by all standing in front of his cage and coughing loudly, and he gladly agreed to go up to Lottie's room for what he called a tactical planning session.

"Situation's becoming a bit desperate, what?" he squeaked, marching up and down Lottie's bedspread. "Time to put on our thinking caps, men! And ladies, of course, so sorry." He bowed to Lottie and Sofie. Sofie sniffed.

"When dealing with an enemy whose forces are

superior — and I mean that only in terms of her experience, dear Lottie — one must resort to underhanded
tactics." Giles nodded happily to himself.

"She's done that already, though, by getting at Ruby,"
Lottie pointed out.

"Espionage. That's what we need," Giles told them
firmly. "A spy network."

"Ruby's lizards are watching her for any clues," Lottie told him. "You mean like that?"

"Excellent, Lottie! You have the makings of an
officer!" Giles gave her an approving nod. "Although
lizards — you know. Not the most reliable chaps.
Always go for a rodent if you can, Lottie. Someone
like Septimus here, or that splendid little lad, Fred.
The pink one. So. When did the lizard squad last
report in?"

"Er, they haven't yet," Lottie admitted, feeling rather
silly.

"Reptiles," Giles muttered irritably. "No sense of
duty. Call them up, Lottie, dear. Demand a status
report!"

"How do I do that?" Lottie muttered to Sofie, trying
not to look stupid in front of Danny and the others.

Try and think lizard, Sofie told her. *Slow your mind
down. Enjoy the sunshine.*

Hey, it's Lottie!

Lottie jumped. That had been easier than she thought. *Hi, Joe. Hi, Sam.*

Lottie, we were just about to try and call you. We think we've got something. Oddly, the lizards seemed to speak together. Lottie wondered if it was to give their voices the strength to cross the distance.

"They've got something for us!" Lottie told the others excitedly.

Ruby's mother keeps wandering around the house looking for a sketchbook. She asked Ruby if she'd borrowed it, but Ruby said no. Her mum's upset because there was lots of stuff in it, work for a big painting she's about to start. And there was a drawing of Ruby, too, that she wanted to frame and give to Ruby's dad for Christmas. We've looked, too, Lottie, and that book isn't anywhere. Someone's taken it.

"Would Pandora be able to use a drawing of Ruby to cast the spell?" Lottie asked Sofie and the others. "One of Ruby's mum's sketchbooks has disappeared." She shuddered. "Ugh, that means she's been in Ruby's house."

She won't be back again, the lizards told her. *We'll make sure of that. But do you think that could be it?*

Sofie nodded. She could hear Joe and Sam too. "It must be that, Lottie. Tell them to keep watching though."

Lottie nodded and said good-bye to the lizards.

"Hey, wait a minute," Danny interrupted her. "Lottie, ask Sam and Joe if there was anything special about that drawing. You never know." He shrugged.

We heard, Sam and Joe told her before she could ask. *It was in pastels. Soft colors. Very good. It looked just like her. She had those hair clips in, the ones you gave her from Paris. That was why Ruby's mother wanted to frame it, because it was just like her. You could feel her in it, more than a photograph. Good-bye, Lottie. We'll keep watch, don't worry.* And they were gone.

"A pastel drawing," Danny said thoughtfully. "Would that work?"

"Could you hear what the lizards were saying too?" Lottie asked in surprise.

Danny blinked. "Um, yes. We all could. We could hear Sam and Joe when they answered you. It just seemed to work like that. I didn't notice we were doing it. They heard me, too, didn't they?" he added thoughtfully.

Lottie nodded slowly. "We ought to be careful. If you can hear me when I'm talking to Sam and Joe, who else can? Do you have all those mind guard things, like Ariadne taught me? If Pandora wants to get at us, she might try you too."

Danny stared at her seriously. "She's tried, Lottie."

"You didn't tell me! Are you OK?" Lottie gave him a worried look.

"I'm not under a spell if that's what you're thinking. Dad told me stuff to do, after Pandora twisted your dreams." He grinned. "I recite soccer stats at her. Works really well — I can feel her getting angry. And I guess us being cousins makes it easier for us to see into each other's minds. I don't think anyone else could break in."

"OK." Lottie nodded. "I suppose so."

Sofie nudged her reassuringly. "Do not worry, Lottie. Pandora does not have the gift with animals that you and Danny share. Her dogs did what she said because they were scared. Not for love. She would not be able to read *our* minds."

Lottie hugged her. *I can't imagine doing this without you*, she told Sofie silently. "So," she added out loud. "Do you think she did steal the drawing? Would that work?"

Giles nodded. "Think about it. A drawing that not only looks like this girl but has the *feel* of her too. And drawn by her mother. It's full of power."

Lottie nodded. "You know, I've just remembered, I've seen that drawing. Ruby's mum showed me it because Ruby had those green clips in her hair, the ones I got

Mum to send. She thought I'd like to see it." Lottie thought carefully for a minute, remembering the sketchbook, then let the others share her memory of the drawing.

"Very like her." Sofie nodded. "Dangerous."

"Do you think her hair makes a difference?" Danny asked, sounding a little embarrassed, as though he thought this was a bit of a girly thing to say.

Everyone stared at him and he blushed. "Well, you know. Those barrette things. If Pandora cast the spell using a picture of Ruby wearing them, with her hair up, does the spell still work if she's got her hair down?"

"Oh!" Lottie tried to think back. "She had those clips in on Friday when she started being weird! Maybe it makes the spell stronger if she looks like the picture."

Giles suddenly stood up on Lottie's bed, looking excited. "Pandora needs the drawing!" he exclaimed. "She wouldn't have bothered to steal it if she didn't, would she? She's left herself open by taking it — we've discovered what she did. She could have just borrowed it. So she must need to have it to keep the spell working." He stared around at them all triumphantly. "So all we have to do is steal it back."

Everyone stared at Giles, not wanting to say it. Finally, Danny muttered, "Oh, so that's all. No problem then."

Giles looked at them, an excited glitter in his little black eyes. "Come on, cheer up! We have a plan. This is excellent."

"Giles, our plan is stealing from an enchantress," Lottie wailed. "It isn't excellent, it's scary!"

"But Lottie, until now we didn't have a plan at all," Giles told her gently, as though speaking to a very small child. "This is a huge step forward."

"Can we step back?" Lottie pleaded. "This isn't a plan, it's a death wish."

"And we know where she lives," Giles pointed out happily. "So we have a plan *and* a location. This is most satisfactory." He actually rubbed his paws together in delight.

"We can't break into her house!" Lottie said in a horrified whisper.

"We could both go into the shop, and one of us will distract her somehow," Danny suggested.

"She is evil, Danny, not stupid," Sofie put in disgustedly.

"We can't just give up," Danny protested. Lottie looked at him nervously. He seemed to have been infected with Giles's enthusiasm, and his eyes had a little of that same crazy gleam.

"There is one time that we could do it," Sofie said slowly, and the others stared at her. She looked up at Lottie and continued reluctantly. "Tonight."

"Tonight?" Lottie squeaked. "Why? Oh! You mean Halloween."

"She will be out on the hills, I am sure," Sofie went on reluctantly. "When we saw her in your dream, that was the place she chose. And she would choose a place where she is powerful to attack you. On Halloween she will be there. Not in that strange little shop."

"Sofie's right." Danny nodded. "Most people like to be outside on Halloween anyway."

"I don't," Lottie said miserably. She didn't want to think about scary Halloween nights. She'd been looking forward to that popcorn. "And what if we're wrong and she hasn't gone out? Or it starts raining and she comes back?"

"You are being very feeble, Lottie," Giles told her disapprovingly.

"I'm only being sensible!" Lottie complained.

"Where is your sense of adventure?" demanded Giles, starting to march up and down her bed again. "Your spirit of derring-do?"

"My what?" Lottie muttered.

"Too much association with reptiles," Giles told Septimus quietly, or at least he thought he was being quiet. "Not a good influence."

"If you want, I'll follow her, Lottie," Danny suggested. Lottie looked up at him in surprise and he shrugged. "Well, you've got Sofie and Giles to help you search the shop. You won't need me. I bet you could get the pink mice to help too. If we watch the shop, I can go after her when she leaves and warn you when it looks like she's coming back."

Lottie nodded. It was a good plan. It was the only plan they had. And she was going to have to go through with it for Ruby's sake, no matter how much she hated the idea. She was going to burglarize a witch's house on Halloween.

7

"Where does Uncle Jack keep the Mouse Elixir?" Lottie asked, searching through the drawers under the counter.

"What do you want that for?" Danny asked from the doorway, where he was keeping watch through a crack. "Still no sign of her."

"I need to bribe Fred and Peach and the others. I can't search a whole house by myself. I know they're only tiny, but there are lots of them. They can help me look. That lot will do anything for Mouse Elixir."

"You're going to take a troop of giggly mice on a top secret mission?" Danny said doubtfully.

"I'm only going to show them the bottle. They can have the elixir when we get back. Oh, here it is!" Lottie pulled out a little brown glass bottle from the back of a drawer and clinked it meaningfully on the counter.

There was a sudden hush as the background noise of scuffling and squeaking that always filled the shop died away. In every cage heads appeared with twitching whiskers. On the top shelf, the seven pink mice stopped playing I Spy (they were fighting because Fred had kept them guessing for ten minutes for something beginning with *K*, and he was refusing to believe that "cat" didn't). They practically vaulted out of their cage and stood in a line on their shelf, staring down at Lottie.

"Would that be your uncle's private stash of elixir, by any chance?" Fred asked casually, but he was wringing his tail in his paws with excitement.

Lottie pulled the stopper out of the bottle, and a waft of pink smoke coiled upward. Every mouse in the shop, and Septimus and Giles, breathed in ecstatically.

"Oh my flourishing whiskers!" Giles muttered. "That's strong stuff."

Lottie jammed the stopper back in.

"Lottie!" protested Peach, Fred's partner in crime. "That's torture. You can't do that! It's cruelty to animals."

"Um, Peach. We aren't regular animals. We can talk," Fred hissed.

"Ssshhh! She doesn't need to know that!" Peach hissed back.

"Er, excuse me?" Lottie broke in politely. "Anyone who wants *a whole thimbleful of Mouse Elixir* can have it later on, if they come out with me tonight."

"A whole thimbleful?" Fred whispered gleefully.

"They'll be dead after a whole thimbleful!" Danny called from the door.

Lottie had seen the effects of Uncle Jack's powerful brew, so she was pretty sure the mice would all be asleep after three sips, but she shrugged. "I'm sure they're all mouse enough to take the risk."

The pink mice were already climbing down the shelves eagerly, but the others were less foolhardy. "Where would we have to go?" a pretty, pink-eyed, white mouse called from her cage.

Lottie eyed the pink mice anxiously and tried to sound casual. "Just down the road." She paused. "To Pandora's shop."

"Where?" the little white mouse squealed. "Are you crazy? Not for a whole bottle!" And she dived into her bedding and curled up in a quivering ball with her tail wrapped around her ears.

The rest of the mice slunk to the back of their cages and pretended they hadn't heard what Lottie said in the first place. There was a sudden clattering of exercise wheels as they all tried to find something to do. But the pink mice, Lottie's favorites, were trooping across the floor and scurrying up her leg to the counter. They formed a worshipful ring around the elixir bottle.

"Are you coming then?" Lottie asked hopefully.

"Of course!" Fred told her. "But Lottie, we do have one very important question."

Lottie nodded. "I know. It *is* going to be risky. I can't deny it. But I promise I'll do my best to keep us all safe."

Fred blinked at her and waved a paw dismissively. "No, no, no. Lottie, listen." He stared up at her and all the others watched them anxiously. "Are we talking about a big thimble or a small one?"

"She's gone!" Danny hissed, and Lottie crept over to the door. They were alone in the shop, apart from the animals. Uncle Jack had gone out an hour before, looking oddly preoccupied. Lottie was feeling even more uneasy about Halloween now. It didn't feel like a special night to her, and she couldn't help worrying in case that meant she was useless at magic. But Danny didn't seem too bothered about it either. Maybe she just had to be older?

It was velvety dark outside. All the streetlamps seemed to have fizzled and faded to nothing. Swirls of mist were coiling along the pavement, but overhead the moon shone high and clear and bright.

A tall figure was moving swiftly down the road, a dark coat wrapped tightly around it.

"Are you sure that's her?" Lottie whispered.

"She came out of the shop. And anyway, look at the hair. She's got the dogs with her too — they're running ahead." Danny pointed out two shadowy shapes floating through the mist farther up the street.

"Oh yes, you're right," Lottie murmured as she saw Pandora flick back her long curtain of white-blond hair.

"Right. I'll follow her." Danny prepared to slide stealthily out of the doorway, but Lottie grabbed his sleeve. "Don't!"

"Lottie! I have to — that's what we planned. Let go, I'll lose her." Danny peered out anxiously again.

"But we don't know what she's gone out to do. Something horrible probably! What if she catches you spying on her? Danny." Lottie gulped. "She might hurt you!"

"Look, I'm not going to get that close to her. I just need to make sure she's still out there and not coming back to the shop. Besides, Lottie, if anything goes wrong, you'll be able to tell, I'm sure you will. Like I could hear you talking to Sam and Joe earlier. Cousins. We're linked, if we want to be." He shot her a fleeting glimpse of himself, looking stubborn. "You can come and help me."

Lottie let go reluctantly. "Just don't do anything stupid," she warned him.

Danny grinned. "I promise." And he slid out into the night, running soft-footed down the road.

Lottie turned back into the shop to find Giles and the mice lined up on the counter. Even the usually silly mice looked almost military. Sofie was perched on the stool behind them, an anxious look in her dark eyes.

"Ready, men?" Giles demanded, and the mice immediately started to twitter and fuss. "Silence! This is a covert mission that must be undertaken with the most extreme discretion!"

The mice all nodded obediently, but the smallest one at the back turned around and muttered to Sofie, "What does that mean?"

Sofie leaned close. "It means *shut up*."

The mouse looked reassured. "I thought it did. I just wanted to check. Are we going now?"

Giles gave Lottie a long-suffering look. "All present and correct!" he reported, sticking his chest out proudly. Lottie thought he would probably have saluted if his paws were long enough.

"OK." Lottie picked up her little backpack. It had lots of pockets, and Giles and the mice climbed in, peeking out over the top. Sofie jumped down from the stool and went to wait by the door. Everyone was quiet and tense, even the mice.

Her heart thudding most uncomfortably, Lottie walked the few yards down the street to Pandora's shop. She had tried to find spells about keys and locks in one of the books Ariadne had lent her, but she hadn't come up with anything useful. However, the mice assured her that she had no need to worry. They would be able to get in with no problem, and they would open the door for her and Sofie and Giles. Or "you fat ones," as they put it.

Outside the shop, Lottie lurked in a side alley while the mice scurried out of her pockets and swarmed up a drainpipe. Lottie could just make them out as they flitted across a low section of roof. Pandora's shop was built in a similar way to Uncle Jack's, all mixed up and squashed together, as though everyone who'd lived there had found it too small and added other pieces. It made it a little worrying in a high wind. The mice were heading for a window that had been left slightly open, and Lottie clapped her hands silently as she saw seven pink tails disappear inside, one after the other.

A couple of minutes later the door swung open eerily and a little pink head poked out of the mail slot. "Hurry up!" squeaked Fred. "This place is horrible."

Lottie had hated the shop yesterday in the daytime;

at night it was a place seen in the worst kind of nightmare. Painted faces leered at them out of the darkness. Lottie closed the door behind them with a dull thud and clicked on her flashlight, dreading what she might see.

A collection of stuffed toys stared back at her with huge glass eyes glowing red in the flashlight beam. Lottie was sure they twitched as she swept the light over them. She turned the flashlight on the counter, but no picture of Ruby was lying on it, as she'd secretly hoped. They would have to go farther in.

"This place has a very bad smell," Sofie whispered.

"I can only smell those disgusting incense sticks," Lottie whispered back. "Can you smell something else?"

Sofie took another cautious sniff. "Bad spells make bad smells," she muttered. "Let us start looking. I want not to be here."

Lottie nodded. "I don't think she would keep it down here," she said thoughtfully. "Although I wouldn't put it past her to frame it and keep it in the shop. No, I think it will be hidden upstairs, or wherever she has her workroom." She stepped bravely toward the door behind the counter, trying to keep the flashlight pointing toward the door and nothing else, but she still couldn't help catching glimpses of odd things as they passed. The china figures whispered in tiny cracked voices, and Lottie had a sudden, horrible thought. What if Pandora had set spies to watch, too, like she and Danny had? What if all these figures, the bears, the puppets, and everything else, could speak to Pandora? What if they were calling her back right now, warning her about an invader? Perhaps Danny had collapsed on the hillside and Pandora was walking down the street, about to corner Lottie in the dark.

Lottie took a deep, steadying breath, feeling the comforting warmth of the mice and Giles all huddling against her neck, their tiny paws wound in her hair.

"Danny will not fail you," Sofie told her, looking back as she approached the door. "If the enchantress is coming back, he *will* tell us."

"I know. I think I just panicked for a moment," Lottie admitted. "This place gives me the creeps."

"It's meant to," Giles pointed out. "The best generals fight with their minds, Lottie. Those toys are all just paint and clay, remember."

Paint and clay and a lot of terrible magic, Lottie thought. But she nodded and they headed up the narrow staircase. Pandora seemed to have spent most of her time organizing and bewitching the shop and so the upper floor was very bare. It made Pandora seem less human, somehow, that she didn't even seem to want cushions or a picture on the wall. Not even a postcard from a friend. Nothing.

"Perhaps it'll be easy to search," Lottie said hopefully. "There's hardly anything here."

But even the barest house still takes a lot of searching, and it was a good half hour later that Lottie sat back on her heels in front of a battered old trunk in the living room and sighed. "I really thought it would have to be in here," she told Sofie. "The kitchen's just like any other kitchen, there's nothing in the bathroom, and only a bed and a closet in the bedroom. I don't know where she does all her spells because I haven't found anything that looks magical, except these books in here." She shut the lid of the trunk gratefully. The books were all bound in dark leather and smelled of mold. They were cold, too, Lottie was sure. Cold seemed to be seeping out of them into the air.

"I should think she does them in her head," Sofie said, peering down the back of the armchair. "No, there is nothing. What do we do now?"

Lottie looked around anxiously. "Try the bedroom again? Perhaps we missed something in the closet. I thought I looked through all those shoe boxes, but I might have lost count."

"You did not lose count." Sofie shook her head. "They were all just shoes. I think she has it with her, this picture."

"Lottie!"

Something sharp in Fred's squeak brought Lottie to her feet at once. "What is it?"

The mice were gathered by another pile of books, large ones, and they'd pulled one off the top of the pile. Lottie had skimmed through them earlier but hadn't found anything that looked like a drawing.

"Oh yes, her photograph album. We're looking for a drawing, though, not a photo. Sorry, Fred."

"Lottie, look at the photo." Fred's voice sounded more serious than she had ever heard him, so Lottie looked, even though she didn't want to. Why would she want to see photos of Pandora? It was horrible enough being in her house. She crouched down next to the mice, who were standing on the album. Sofie nosed her way in too. They all stared down at the photograph.

At last Giles cleared his throat. "Ahem! That looks rather like your uncle, Lottie."

Lottie shook her head. "No." Her voice was very quiet. "It isn't my uncle. It's my father."

"With Pandora," Sofie whispered, and Lottie nodded.

They were a couple, it was easy to see. Lottie's dad had his arm around her, and she was looking up at him. They looked so happy.

"They're very young," Fred said comfortingly. "It must have been a long time ago, Lottie."

"Why didn't anyone tell me?" Lottie muttered. "Are there any more pictures of them?"

The mice turned the pages and found several more photos of Lottie's dad. There they were, sitting by the fountain in the park, and there, leaning against the parapet of the bridge over the river.

"They were here," Lottie said blankly. "These were all taken around here."

"She said that she had lived here before," Sofie reminded her.

"Take it out," Lottie said to Fred. "That first one. Pull it out of the album."

"If you do that, Lottie, she'll know we've been here," Giles warned her.

"She'll know anyway." Lottie looked around the bare, miserable little room. "She'll know. She'll be able to feel me. She'll feel how angry I am. Come on. We're going to Ariadne's. I want to know what really happened, and Uncle Jack won't tell me. I'm not going to let them sweet-talk me again."

*   *   *

Lottie hammered on the door of Ariadne's apartment, impatient and angry. Catching her mood, Sofie scrabbled anxiously at the door with her paws.

It didn't open.

"I suppose we should have expected they'd be out tonight," Lottie said, the anger suddenly disappearing and leaving her limp and tired. She sat down on the stairs, her eyes filling with weary tears.

Sofie, Giles, and the mice swarmed into her lap. Sofie gently licked away Lottie's tears and the mice crooned comfort and compliments as they scurried around her shoulders. Giles climbed to the top of her backpack and perched there, trying to cheer her up.

"Very difficult situation to be in, Lottie, old thing. Worrying." Seeing that it wasn't working, he dropped the happy voice for a moment and looked her straight in the eye. "Just remember, Lottie. It's *you* that matters. Your choices, what you do. Not what your parents did before you were even thought of."

Lottie sniffed and nodded. "I know. But I still want to understand. I mean . . . how could he?" She leaned her head against the wall and closed her eyes. The photograph was in one of the pockets of her backpack, but she didn't need to see it. She felt as though it was burned onto her brain. The way they looked at each other. Could she remember her parents ever looking at each other like that?

"Are we staying here, Lottie?" Sofie asked gently.

Lottie nodded, not speaking. Then she murmured, "Sorry. You can go back to the shop if you're tired. I want to wait for Ariadne."

"Do not be so foolish," Sofie told her sternly. "We are not leaving you. But we ought to tell Danny that he can go home too."

Lottie opened her eyes wide. "Oh! I forgot about Danny!"

"I thought you had," Sofie said rather smugly. "Do not worry, I have told him now. He — oh! He is coming here. He says you should not wait on your own. But you are not on your own, Lottie, you are with me. He is a silly boy, that one."

Danny thundered up the stairs five minutes later. "Did you get it?" he asked hopefully.

Lottie blinked at him. "Oh . . . the drawing. No, I think she must have it on her."

Danny glared. "Yes, of course, the drawing. The whole point of the evening. What's up with you, Lottie? You look like you've seen a ghost." He grinned to himself, but then he looked at Lottie again and his smile faded.

Fred and Peach carefully pulled the photo out of the backpack and Danny stared at it. "That's . . . that's Uncle Tom, isn't it?" he said at last. "I don't really remember him, but it doesn't look quite like Dad, so it must be. With *her.*"

"Exactly." The cool smoothness of the wall against her cheek was comforting, and Lottie didn't want to think anymore. She was vaguely aware that Danny was talking to Sofie, but it didn't seem very important. Nothing seemed very important anymore.

"Lottie! Lottie!"

Lottie blinked dazedly and looked up. Ariadne was sitting on the step next to her, an arm around her shoulders. Tabitha and Shadow were on either side of her, their green eyes glowing like jewels in the darkness of the stairway.

"Did you see it?" Lottie murmured, gazing up at her. "The photo?"

"Yes, I did. Come on, Lottie, come inside. It's freezing out on these stairs. Your poor mice are practically purple with cold." She lifted Lottie up and led her into the apartment, settling her and Danny at the kitchen table and starting up her enormous coffee machine. "It's all right, Lottie, I'll make hot chocolate for you, but I need coffee to deal with this and so does Sofie."

Lottie nodded. "Oh! The mice! I promised them Mouse Elixir. You don't have any, do you?"

The mice, who had been watching Ariadne's coffee machine with great interest, now stared up at her hopefully.

Ariadne looked doubtful. "No. I have some Cowslip Syrup that one of my aunts gave me. It's at the back of a cupboard somewhere."

"That would do," Fred said swiftly.

Ariadne didn't have any thimbles, either, but the mice assured her politely that they would drink out of egg cups, no problem at all.

The hot chocolate was very sweet and comforting and Lottie felt much better after only a couple of sips. "What did you put in this?" she asked Ariadne suspiciously, watching the pink steam rising from her cup and coiling in delicate patterns toward the ceiling.

"Ask me no questions and I'll tell you no lies," Shadow growled. He was very protective of his mistress. "A saying you'd do well to remember, Lottie."

"Ssshhh, Shadow." Ariadne stroked his head. "Lottie, don't worry, it's just essence of roses. It's an old recipe, that's all. No magic. Well, only a little. It's only to make you feel a bit better."

"I don't want to feel better!" Lottie snapped, banging her mug down on the table. "I want everybody to stop pretending and tell me what's really going on. I've seen the proof. You can't lie to me anymore."

"Did Uncle Tom really go out with that . . . that . . ." Danny trailed off.

"Pandora?" Ariadne sighed. "Yes, he did. For five years. They were childhood sweethearts. Everyone thought they'd be together forever."

"They really loved each other?" Lottie asked in a small voice.

Ariadne nodded, looking at Lottie sympathetically. "I know you don't want to hear it, Lottie, but yes. They were so close. That's why it hit them so hard when it went wrong."

"What happened?" Lottie demanded. "Did you know them all then?"

"Ariadne was my mum's best friend," Danny explained.

Ariadne shrugged. "Pandora's magic happened. The mind-twisting stuff she does. Tom closed his eyes to it for a long while. He couldn't admit to himself what she was doing, you see. Jack spoke to him about it eventually, pointed out that she was going too far. Tom was furious. He hit Jack and knocked him out. That's when he realized, when he saw his brother stretched out on the floor. She'd been doing it to him too. She knew Jack didn't like her, and she'd been trying to turn Tom against him. She'd forgotten they were brothers. She was an only child herself, and I don't think she understood the power of that bond. He ended it after that." Ariadne sighed. "He told her she had to stop, that she was going bad. Of course, the sad thing is, by breaking up with her, he turned her completely."

"And then he met my mum?" Lottie asked.

"A few months after, yes." Ariadne smiled. "They were so different, Isobel and Pandora. To be honest, Lottie, I think that was one of the things that your dad liked about her right away."

Lottie shook her head. "Ever since I got here, I couldn't think how he could marry someone who didn't understand magic. I suppose that was why."

"Yes, but he didn't just go out and find the first non-magical girl he could, Lottie. He swore for a while that he'd never let himself love anyone, in case they did that to him again." Ariadne took a sip of coffee and grinned, remembering. "He resisted your mum as hard as he could, but she bewitched him even more than Pandora had, without any magic at all."

"Was Pandora still around?" Danny asked. "I can't see her giving up easily somehow."

"She couldn't believe he'd broken up with her." Ariadne shivered. "She wasn't as strong then as she is now, but she was powerful enough to be a dangerous enemy. Especially for someone like Isobel, who had no idea what she really was. She kept on trying, too, over the years. Even though she'd moved away from Netherbridge, every so often Tom would get a letter from her, or he'd go around looking ill for a few days, and you'd know she'd had another go at his mind. But he loved your mum so much, Pandora could never twist his thoughts away from her."

Lottie was amazed by the sudden surge of protective love she felt for her mother at the thought of Pandora attacking her. "Did she hurt my mum?" she demanded.

"She tried. And she tried to tell your mum about the magic too. Isobel thought she was crazy." Ariadne sighed. "It would have been funny if it weren't so sad. The odd thing is, I'm sure Pandora could have killed Isobel if she'd tried hard enough. But that didn't seem to be what she wanted. I suppose killing her wouldn't have gotten Tom back. And Pandora was more subtle than that. I do wonder . . ." she trailed off.

"What?" Lottie glared at her. "Come on, Ariadne, what were you going to say?"

Ariadne looked at her thoughtfully. "I wonder whether Isobel would have accepted the idea of magic one day if it hadn't been for Pandora. Pandora closed her mind to it entirely. I think Tom always hoped that she would understand eventually, especially when you were born. But it never happened. I mean, you saw what your mum was like when she came here again — she had no idea. She didn't remember that she'd met me before, even. It's as though that time is gone for her."

Lottie blinked as she imagined the life she would have had if her mother had understood about magic. She wouldn't have taken Lottie away from here, surely, if she'd known. She wouldn't have felt so alone in Netherbridge that she had to leave. And Lottie's dad might not have wanted to go off on his unbelievably ridiculous search for unicorns if her mum had understood him better. Lottie dug her fingernails into her palms to stop herself from howling as she finally understood what Pandora had taken away from her.

Then she gasped. Unbelievably stupid. Far too stupid to believe . . .

"What is it?" Ariadne asked her anxiously. "Lottie, sweetheart, what's wrong?"

"The unicorns! When my dad disappeared, Uncle Jack said he went to search for unicorns in the rain forest somewhere and he never came back."

"Unicorns! That's a fairy tale!" Danny laughed, and then looked immediately sorry as he saw Lottie's face.

"I know! It was crazy. My dad was obsessed enough about them to leave me and my mum even when she didn't want him to go." She looked around at them all. "Don't you see? It wasn't real! Pandora got to him at last. She planted it in his mind, I know she did. She stopped trying to get my dad back, but she couldn't stand for my mother to win. She didn't kill my mum, she killed him instead. So no one could have him if she couldn't."

"Lottie, you can't be sure of that," Ariadne began soothingly.

"Don't you think it's true?" Lottie demanded, fixing her eyes on Ariadne's.

Ariadne faltered. "I — I don't know, Lottie. It did seem a strange thing for him to do. I remember thinking so at the time, when your aunt told me. But then, I remember he always was a bit odd about unicorns. He wanted to believe in them so much. They were one of his favorite dreams."

"Pandora would have known that too," Lottie said quietly. "She would have known just how to trick him. I know I can't prove it. But I'm sure, really, really sure. As soon as I thought of it, I could feel it was true." She was silent for a moment, then she looked up at Ariadne and Danny again. "She didn't know about me, did she? She bit her lip so hard she drew blood when Uncle Jack told her I wasn't his daughter. Did she never know that my mum and dad had a baby?"

"She'd gone away, hadn't she?" Danny asked. "Before you were born. She might not have found out."

"She tried to attack me in that dream the same night she found out who I was," Lottie remembered. "She asked if I wanted to be her apprentice instead of yours, Ariadne. She wants my dad's child under her control."

"Or dead," Danny added. Everyone glared at him and he shrugged. "Sorry, Lottie, but I figure it's true. She's crazy."

Lottie drank the last of her chocolate and stood up, reaching for her coat.

"Are you going home?" Ariadne asked, slightly surprised.

Lottie wrapped her scarf around her neck thoughtfully. "No. I'm going back to Pandora's shop. I want to talk to her."

"What?" Ariadne, Sofie, and Danny all spoke at once.

"Lottie, you can't! You don't know what could happen." Ariadne got up and took her hands. "And in her shop, in her territory, she'll have the advantage. She'll break down your defenses."

"No she won't. Or maybe she will, I don't know. I'm not just going to go home and pretend this didn't happen. She killed my dad, Ariadne!" Lottie's voice shook.

"You can't go after her in this state," Shadow pronounced.

"She can't do it at all!" Ariadne told him angrily.

"She has to," Sofie whispered. "Lottie is right. But not tonight. Wait till tomorrow, Lottie."

"It won't be any easier to fight her tomorrow." Ariadne gave Lottie a little shake. "This is craziness."

Lottie laughed, trembling. "Well, she's crazy, too, isn't she? We'll be even. I have to, like Sofie said. I can't not. You told me once that there was no point in having magic if I wouldn't use it. This is when I need to use it, Ariadne. Now or never."

Ariadne looked at her. "Maybe you are ready," she said quietly. "Do you want me to come with you?"

Lottie shook her head. She did, actually, but she had a strong feeling that she had to do this on her own. She'd wondered about asking Danny to come, but she didn't want her big cousin along to look after her. Much. She had a sudden thought and looked anxiously at Sofie.

"Of course I am coming," the little dog told her irritably. "But we are definitely waiting until tomorrow. Night is Pandora's time, not ours. She is the one who needs the dark."

Lottie smiled at her. "Mmm. We're definitely sunshine witches."

Ariadne put her hands on Lottie's shoulders. "I think Sofie is right that you shouldn't go now. You're too upset, too angry. But remember the anger, and use it, Lottie! Control it, make sure it doesn't control you. Don't let it die down." Her voice was quiet and sad as she added, "You're very strong, Lottie, stronger than you realize. But you're going to need everything you've got against Pandora."

Lottie shivered. It was hard to believe that she was about to confront a powerful enchantress, with only a small dog for company.

The next morning, Lottie woke up with the same strange, anxious feeling that she sometimes got before a big test at school. At first she couldn't remember why, but then she saw Sofie lying on the duvet next to her with her paws in the air and snoring gently. All at once it flooded back. She was a witch who'd inherited her magic from her father. He'd been destroyed by another witch, an evil one, and today Lottie was going to fight for him.

The temptation to turn over and go back to sleep was very strong.

"Sofie," she whispered.

Sofie opened one eye sleepily and then shook her

ears. "I think this is a good day for chocolate before breakfast, Lottie, hmmm?"

Lottie grinned. "You're probably right. In fact, maybe we ought to have some chocolate and then get dressed quickly and grab a couple of slices of toast. Uncle Jack doesn't usually open the shop on Sundays, so he'll be sleeping in, and I shouldn't think Danny's planning to get up at all. I don't want Uncle Jack asking us questions about where we're going."

Sofie shook her head. "No. You are not a very good liar, Lottie. It is something we should work on. I do not think your uncle will be down for a while though. He was probably out on Netherbridge Hill last night, looking for that unicorn."

Lottie shuddered. "I hope he didn't meet Pandora."

They crept downstairs to make toast and then sat looking at each other over the crumbs.

"Shall we go?" Lottie said, taking a deep breath, which was difficult. Her chest seemed to have become very tight.

"Mmmm." Sofie licked the last drops of coffee out of her pink china bowl. *"Allons-y.* I mean, let us go, Lottie. You must learn more French," she said sternly in response to Lottie's blank look.

"I promise I will," Lottie told her.

It felt strange to walk down the street with only Sofie in her arms. Lottie felt as though she ought to be more prepared.

Pandora wasn't in the shop, but the door opened when Lottie pushed it, so she and Sofie simply walked inside. The silvery bell tinkled, its notes ringing horribly in Lottie's ears.

Sofie shook her head irritably. "That bell is . . . is *wrong*!" she pronounced.

"It's a spell bell!" Lottie said, giggling foolishly.

Sofie gave her a sharp look but Lottie stopped laughing. "It's all right, I'm just nervous. It wasn't a spell."

Another door at the back of the shop opened and Pandora walked in, a wary look on her face. The door obviously led to the backyard, and she was carrying a bunch of herbs. The odd, bitter smell reached as far as Lottie was standing, and Sofie sneezed.

Pandora smiled thinly. She didn't seem too surprised to see them. The salukis slid through the door past Pandora and let out a low, throbbing growl, hardly more than a breath.

"Be careful, Sofie!" Lottie warned.

"They do not scare me!" Sofie hissed.

"I know, that's why I'm worried!" Lottie put a firm hand on Sofie's collar.

The little dog is very brave, Lottie. A silky voice was filling her head, and it made her shudder. *But you aren't quite so brave, are you?*

"I'm here, aren't I?" Lottie snapped back, out loud. She didn't want Pandora in her head.

"But you're shaking, Lottie, and your heart is beating so fast," Pandora purred. "Yes, I can feel it, you know. I'm inside you already, and I could put my hand around your heart and squeeze it lifeless in a second."

"That's not true!" Lottie tried to sound confident, but all at once she was sure she could feel Pandora's fingers creeping through her veins and Pandora's breath in her throat. She was choking!

Lottie, stop! If you believe it, then it is so! Listen, Lottie, she is lying to you!

Sofie's angry little voice broke the spell and Lottie's head snapped up. She shook her dark curls out of her eyes angrily and saw Pandora wince.

Now! Now! Sofie snapped, and together their thoughts surged toward Pandora in her moment of weakness.

Her mind was a seething mass of bitterness. *So like her father. Same eyes, those same black curls. He betrayed me, and he paid for it. She'll pay, too, the worthless little brat! But she's strong. I'll have her power. Make her mine.*

She'd discovered Lottie and Sofie, and in a furious burst of anger she flung them out of her mind.

Pandora was so strong it was like being struck by lightning. A burst of white light exploded behind Lottie's eyes, and it was followed by cold blackness. Lottie tried to open her eyes and found that they were already open. The darkness was still there. She knew she was Lottie — or was she? She thought she was. But she knew nothing else. Not where, or who, or how.

Perhaps she should close her eyes again and go to sleep? There seemed nothing else to do, after all. . . . And if she closed her eyes, that horrible blackness might go away.

"Lottie!" It was a bark and it shattered the blackness into a thousand tiny diamonds. Lottie was lying on the floor of the shop, curled up into a ball, with Sofie staring at her.

Lottie blinked. "Why's there a hamster on your head?"

The hamster leaned forward. "It's me, Lottie, old thing. Giles. I, er, had to wake Sofie up. She woke you. Very powerful bark she has there."

"He bit me," Sofie said pathetically, holding up one paw.

"Did you follow us?" Lottie asked. She was starting to feel a bit more like herself.

"No, I was in your pocket the whole time. Felt you needed some backup. The reserves, you know. Not good to show the entire force to the enemy."

Lottie made a small noise that sounded like *eep!* "Pandora! I'd forgotten her. Where is she?"

"I think it wore her out when she threw that light at us," Sofie explained. "But we have not got long, I think." She nodded over at the counter. Pandora, seated, was leaning against it with the salukis nosing at her face. Even as Sofie spoke, she stared over at Lottie and stood up, pushing the dogs away. They whined softly and she snarled at them to be quiet.

"You can tell what someone's like from the way they treat animals." It was something Uncle Jack often said. Lottie realized it was true as she said it.

"So noble. Your father's daughter, Lottie. Tom was noble too. That's why he was so obsessed with those stupid unicorns. He thought they were the noblest creatures ever to have lived."

"It *was* you who sent him after them, then." Lottie clenched her fists.

"Of course. You know it was. I heard some ridiculous rumor and I made sure it got to Tom. I knew how he'd take it. Then I arranged for him to encounter some . . . friends of mine while he was out there."

"You killed him!"

"Oh yes, Lottie. And I'd do it again, in a heart-beat." Pandora's purring laugh filled the shop and filled Lottie's mind in a swirl of anger and hate. She dimly heard Sofie barking again and Giles crying, "Lottie, no! Don't let her do this to you!" But Lottie wasn't there anymore. She was lost in a fire of fury and revenge.

I've won! I've won! A triumphant whisper filled Lottie's ears and she turned, twisting, her eyes burning. Where was she? Pandora had trapped her again, and she couldn't feel Sofie or Giles.

I got too caught up in my anger, Lottie told herself miserably. *She's made me like her. It's what Ariadne told me not to do. That's why she wouldn't let me come here last night. Oh, I've been so stupid!*

Pandora's whisper was now a painful cry in Lottie's mind. *You certainly have. And now I have you and I can use you, Lottie, darling. Your mother, your irritatingly disapproving uncle. Your cousin. I'll get to them all through you. Just like I used your little friend.*

Lottie shook her head desperately. *No! I won't let you! Oh help, someone help me!*

There isn't anyone, Pandora snapped. But Lottie detected just a thread of unease in her voice and she called again. *Help, help me, please!*

All at once the redness seemed to cool and another voice was there.

You only had to call, Lottie. I'll always come. And the white unicorn was standing at her shoulder, facing Pandora with her, and Sofie had leaped into her arms and was licking her cheek lovingly.

You! Pandora screamed, and Lottie gasped.

She knew who the unicorn was.

It was her father.

"Lottie! Lottie, wake up!"

Lottie gasped and jumped awake.

"Oh, thank goodness, I thought you were dead!" Ruby hugged her. "Are you all right?"

Lottie looked around. She was still in the shop, but there was no sign of Pandora or the unicorn. Sofie was curled in her lap, looking as confused as she felt, and Giles was standing on the shop counter staring around anxiously.

"No sign!" he reported. "She got away, I think."

"Lottie . . ." Ruby looked around the shop, her eyes bewildered. "Lottie, was the woman who ran this place a *witch*?"

"Of course she was!" Sofie snapped. "And you have a lot of apologizing to do. You have been most unpleasant. You deserved to be bitten!"

"Sofie, that isn't fair," Lottie protested. "Ruby was under a spell."

"Was I?" Ruby muttered. "That explains things. I can't remember anything about the past week. Just these odd flashes here and there. Then I found myself standing outside this shop, and I saw you lying on the floor."

"Ruby, I met my dad!" Lottie's eyes were shining with excitement. "Only in a sort of dream, and he was a unicorn, but it was him. He's not dead." She looked uncertainly at Sofie. "At least I don't think he can be."

Sofie shrugged. "I do not know. He felt real. But it could have been a memory, perhaps?"

"Your dad's a *horse*?" Ruby asked, staring at her.

Lottie grinned at her tiredly. "Don't look at me like that. Let's go home. I promise I will explain. I just can't work it all out myself right now. Please come back with me?"

Ruby nodded, still looking dazed. She pulled Lottie up and Lottie staggered to her feet, clutching Sofie, and Giles jumped onto her shoulder. "Lottie, manners!" he whispered as they walked out into the sunshine. "Introduce this young lady!"

"Oh yes. Ruby, this is Giles. He's a hamster. Giles, this is Ruby." Lottie put an arm around her. "She's my best friend."

Pay another visit to Grace's Pet Shop!

There's more magic in store!

The pet shop was in a row of little shops: a rather dingy café advertising all-you-can-eat breakfasts served all day; the sort of hardware shop that sells absolutely everything, all tucked away on hundreds and hundreds of tiny shelves; and a shop that sold knitting wool, with a window full of ugly sweaters.

The door squeaked shrilly as it swung open, and a dank smell of grubby cages rushed out at them, making Lottie grimace.

No one was sitting behind the counter, so the girls wandered around, poking into piles to see if there was anything they could use for warming up lizards in them.

"What are we actually looking for?" Lottie asked, holding a pink fluffy cat coat in dismay. No self-respecting cat would be seen dead in it. "Sort of lizard hot-water bottles?"

"I don't know," Ruby said thoughtfully. "I thought a new heat lamp for their tank — they're like artificial sunlight, you know? But Sam said what he'd really like were hot stones that he could lie on. I don't know if you can even buy those. I've a feeling that the sort of lizard they are might be used to living quite close to volcanoes."

Sam and Joe hadn't told Ruby they were actually dragons yet. Lottie thought they didn't want to upset her. Besides, with all their research into flame production, she might be a bit worried about them living in her bedroom.

"What do you two want?" snapped a grumpy voice, making Lottie jump and knock over a stack of chew toys and a plastic Scottie wearing a plaid dog coat. She scooped them up guiltily, while a little old lady with a sour, pinched face glared at them both.

Ruby started to explain what they were looking for, while the old lady alternated between grumbling about how much she hated reptiles and glaring at Lottie.

"We've got nothing like that. Lot of nonsense," she muttered, when Ruby finished her halting description.

Ruby sighed and was just turning to leave, when something in the tottering pile behind the old woman's head caught her eye. "Oh, but look! Reptile sun lamp! You do have one, up there!" she pointed out.

With much complaining, the old woman fetched a stepstool and started to reach for the lamp. Lottie, having already knocked over one pile, decided the best thing to do was stay out of the way. She retreated back away from the counter to look at a shelf full of mouse bedding and came face to face with a rabbit.

Or rather, face to bottom. The rabbit's cage (which looked horribly small for him) was tucked away on a big shelf between the mouse bedding and stones for the bottom of fish tanks. He was facing into one corner, looking at the wall. Lottie immediately got the sense that he wasn't happy.

"Hey," she whispered, and the rabbit twitched a little. But he stayed staring at the wall. "Are you all right?" Lottie wasn't sure if she was expecting the rabbit to answer. Surely they wouldn't have magical creatures in this grim place? The rabbit peered over his shoulder hopelessly, his eyes dull. He blinked at the sight of Lottie, and his ears wiggled slightly. A faint gleam shone in his eyes, and he put his head on one side thoughtfully. Then he shuffled round so that he was looking at her properly.

"Do you — like it here?" Lottie asked, waving a hand at the dusty piles of stuff around his cage.

The rabbit gave her an expressive look. *What do you think?* he seemed to be saying.

Lottie nodded. "It's pretty awful, isn't it. . . ?" she murmured.

"Don't bother the animals!" the old woman shouted across the shop. "I won't have the likes of you upsetting them. You ought to be ashamed of yourself!"

"Me!" Lottie shot back, whirling around. She stalked back over to the counter. "I'm not upsetting him! He's miserable, can't you tell? He was just staring at the wall! He shouldn't be in a tiny little cage like that anyway."

"You mind your own business!" the old woman snapped.

"Cruelty to animals is everyone's business," Lottie told her. She had no idea where she was going with this. She didn't have enough money to buy the rabbit, and she was sure that the rabbit wasn't actually being badly treated enough that she could report the shop to the SPCA or anywhere like that. He was just miserable.

"Cruelty! Right. Both of you, out of my shop, this minute. Cheeky little devils, I'll have the police on you!" And the old woman surged round the counter in a rush and hurried them out, squawking and gobbling like an angry, scrawny-necked chicken.

As she bustled them out of the door, Lottie looked back and saw the rabbit sadly turning around to face the wall again. That one glance back decided it.

She was going to get him out of there.

Unfortunately, she had absolutely no idea how.

Run, fly, or swim down to Grace's Pet Shop.

Lottie is happy to spend her time talking to the animals in her uncle's pet shop. Then one day, to her surprise, the animals start to talk back!

School is definitely more fun now that Lottie has best friend, Ruby. But what will her new friend do if she finds out Lottie has magical powers?

How can one Pet cause ト

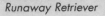

Chapter Books

Runaway Retriever

Loudest Beagle on the Block

Mud-Puddle Poodle

Bulldog Won't Budge

Oh No, Newf!

••• Read the series and find out! •••

A new neighbor is in town, with magic stronger than Lottie's and a mind to make trouble. Lucky for Lottie, the pet shop's newest resident, Giles the hamster, is ready to help.

Lottie has discovered an unhappy rabbit at a dingy pet shop. He seems to have budding magical abilities and Lottie is determined to rescue him!

Magic is everywhere
and all the animals can talk!